The Tactics of Love
Guardians of Refuge Book 3
Alyssa Bailey

This book is all about...

Marine Lt. Colonel Darrell, "Chopper" Frazier spent most of his adult life in the military as a special operations pilot. He is known for his uncanny ability to get in and get out of the roughest tactical situations. He loved flying and the adrenaline thrill that accompanied the high-risk job. But, after spending hours with Felicity "Doc" Torrez, MD, he knew what he was missing, so when the time to get out arrived, he was ready to find Felicity and see if they had a future.

Felicity wasn't sorry she had left the Army but starting over in the civilian world was complicated. Adjusting to a different culture was challenging and isolating. She left the Army to start a family; unfortunately, it wasn't as easy as it sounded. After every unsuccessful date, her mind would return to that Marine Pilot who she met on her last night in-country and how he made her feel safe and happy.

Quite by accident, they find each other again and begin to explore their attraction and mesh their goals. But, even as they are planning their days ahead together, someone has an entirely different future for Felicity. Chopper will need the help of his SEAL friends and associates to find Felicity before it's too late.

Love the inside scoop? Sign up for my Newsletter with special offers and bonus content.

https://www.alyssabaileyromance.com

Prologue

Felicity signed herself out of the field clinic for the last time. She was leaving in the morning, going back to the States. She had served her rotation, and it hadn't been as easy or as complicated as she had thought, but there was a sense of pride whenever she rotated out of an overseas stint. But to be honest with herself, she was lonely and feeling a little burnout after this assignment.

Unlike other deployments, hers rarely lasted longer than six months at a time. Still, if she had started a family during that time, it would have been hard. Single, she didn't have to worry about being gone too much, working odd hours, or taking someone's rotation so they could get a little more time with their loved ones.

Recently, Felicity had been thinking of the family life she put on hold. She wanted a couple of children and a husband. On the downside of thirty, it occupied her thoughts more and more, but she was not starting a family without a husband. Blame her old-fashioned ideas, but she wanted a husband that took care of her and their family. Possessively. Protectively. Lovingly. And though it was difficult, she acknowledged it might not happen for her.

With that goal in mind, she had thrown out some feelers for jobs she might like. Finding a new job for a physician differed from applying to the want ads; however, she found it wasn't much different. She didn't have a place she called home to go back to and join a practice or hospital. Her parents moved from where she had grown up in the Olympia Washington area to Oregon. Besides, her family had all gone on to the next stage of their lives, so should she.

Felicity wasn't sure what direction she wanted to go or where she wanted to take herself and her practice. Her vision, so clear for all of her adult life, now wavered. The Army had been good for her, but she no longer wanted to stay. Maybe something she liked, something that grabbed her imagination, would pop up, and the next stage of her life could begin. Felicity turned to smile a last goodbye to the desk clerk, who held his hand up while finishing his phone call.

"Major, we have two field medics trying to patch up more people than they have a hope of doing. They are asking for help, and there isn't any right now, Ma'am. Chopper heard the request. He was close and said he would be wheels up in ten minutes. He can take you out there."

"I'm officially off duty because I'm leaving tomorrow, but I can at least help stabilize. Is the place safe to work in?" She knew that was rhetorical, but the petty officer answered, anyway.

"Safe, Ma'am? Um..." The clerk raised his eyebrows.

"That's what I thought." Felicity sighed. Guess that last farewell to the others would have to wait.

She should really let Colonel Richie know of the situation. He was her boss here in this multi-service base for one more night. The man hated things going outside of plan and protocol. Felicity wondered how he had lasted so long in the military or as a doctor. Those were the realities of life every day. Hell, any military member had to be very flexible.

"Let Chopper know I'm on my way. Call Colonel Richie and let him know."

She rushed out, not waiting to hear the Petty Officer's response. She'd heard the typical "yes, ma'am" so often in the last decade, her brain rarely acknowledged it anymore. She'd decided to join the Army soon after she had decided to become a doctor. When she was accepted to medical school, she took the military scholarship and stayed Army after completing her four-year commitment.

Felicity's mind was racing as she tried to imagine what situation would meet her when she arrived. She liked her own gear, but she had nothing in her quick, already packed go-bag that the medics and techs wouldn't already have. That being the case, she sprinted to the airfield.

A tall, fit man was standing next to a helicopter, so she headed his way. It wasn't anything new to see big, brawny, or athletic men in the military. Tall, short, average men were universally in top form and were nice eye candy. There were so many. Her brain was saturated, and like the answer from the petty officer, she rarely noticed.

But today was an exception. This pilot was a legend. He typically flew for special ops because he had a reputation of getting in the rough spots and doing extractions others wouldn't attempt. Felicity had admired him both professionally and as a man from afar. She bet he didn't have a family waiting for him at home, either. She indulged in a moment's fantasizing about what it would be like to come home to him.

Chopper had muscles that his rolled sleeves could barely contain. He didn't smile, and he had those stereotypical mirrored shades. His jaw clenched firmly, and his angular face was so hard, Felicity expected the stress to crack and shatter his good looks. Handsome in a rough, angry sort of way, he shouldn't appeal to her. She always looked for a gentle lover because her job was rough enough, but something about him pulled at her.

Her belly tightened, and she felt a brief flutter in her lady bits. Felicity knew the clinical terms, but she had learned a long time ago that if it wasn't another doctor, and sometimes not even then, no one liked clinical descriptions when you were trying to get in each other's pants. It wasn't sexy, and it definitely killed the mood.

But Felicity wasn't getting in the mood for anything but going stateside. That she was having a hot flash moment over Chopper was ridiculous and spoke to how much she felt the weight of working so many hours over the last months. He was here to do a job just like she was, and that was all. Even so, she couldn't help but take one last look before stepping closer to the transport.

He'd already fired the helicopter up. The noise was loud, and the wind it kicked up threw small particles of dirt and debris in the surrounding air. Felicity tried to shield her eyes, but it didn't help much. The serious pilot put his hand on her head and bent her down to a half-crouch without speaking. He mimicked her stance as he hustled her into the bird. She was fumbling with the seatbelt when he hopped up into the pilot seat and put a headset on her head. Suddenly, she could hear him loudly.

"You the doc?"

"I'm Major Torrez, yes."

"I'm Chopper. Only two rules when riding with me," he said as he reached over and settled her belt before he rapidly flipped and checked gauges, switches, and the surrounding perimeter.

"What are they?" She was a little excited to be riding in a helicopter. It had been years, and she loved the freedom being in one gave her. Someone usually provided her with ground transport.

"The first one is: follow the boss's orders." Chopper seemed satisfied with his checks, and Felicity listened in on his conversation between the tower and him.

She watched as he made the giant flying machine rise straight up in the air. Her belly dropped into her shoes like a fast elevator. Only this expensive machine went up and then off to an angle. Felicity tried to grab onto something but ended up holding her safety strap tightly. She had to hand it to him; he was an expert pilot. He relaxed, and she could see, even though he must have made thousands of trips, he was enjoying the flight.

"And the second rule?" asked Felicity. She never could leave things unsaid, but she really wanted to know the answer in this case.

"Right." He turned and gave her the first semblance of a smile that grew into a boyish grin. "I'm the boss."

A laugh burst from her lips, and she just realized she hadn't mentally noted his rank. That was out of character for her. She tried to remedy that when Chopper looked back over at her and grinned again.

"Both majors for a few more weeks, so that means I'm the boss."

She smiled back because his grin was contagious. "How do you figure?"

"It's my bird." He glanced back at the scenery in front of them and nodded ahead. "Be about twenty more mins, so tell me about yourself."

No one ever asked Felicity personal questions. Usually, her co-workers weren't interested in anything more than surface information, or there wasn't time. They all had lives to return to, and that was their primary goal. Get the job done and get home. She'd learned long ago that any connection in a war zone was not a good idea. Yes, trust each other professionally, but any other, deeper commitments weren't likely. The special ops teams were different, but not the medical corps.

"Nothing much to tell, really. I'm a doctor, and I'm about to resign from my commission in a few months. What about you?"

"Whoa, you're leaving the military? Why? I thought docs had it cushy." He glanced her way as though seeing her in a new light.

"I'm tired, burned out, lonely, and want a change. Besides, being a woman in the Army is a hard thing, regardless of your MOS." She had already bared her soul to a man she had never met before, except by reputation. What was that all about?

He gave her an assessing stare. "You aren't one of those discrimination screamers, are you? Because I can put this bird right down and–"

"What, no, I just... look, I said too much. Ignore me. I'm rotating stateside tomorrow because my deployment is up. I'll go to Hood and then, from there, will probably give my notice, so to speak."

"Again, why?" Chopper was serious now and seemed interested in her answer.

She shrugged and looked out her window. "It's time for a new direction. I'd like a family before it's too late. I'm not the type of person who can leave her babies thousands of miles at home while I work in another location for months at a time. It's time to put down roots, plant a tree and see it grow."

"Yes, I get that. The military doesn't give us much in the way of family stability. It used to, but that was in my dad's time, not mine."

"Do you have a family?" The thought that he might have a wife and maybe kids made sense, but she selfishly hoped he didn't.

"Nah. I've seen how hard it is to stay a functional family with your service member deployed so often. When I marry, if I marry, I'm going to expect it to last, and that means no more special ops, so that's likely when I'm done with the military."

"And when do you think that could be?"

"I'm coming up on retirement now, but I took this rank, so as long as I can continue doing what I love, then I'll stay. When it's no longer fulfilling, then I'll go."

They were silent for the remainder of the trip until the outpost came into view. Chopper pointed to the group of tents and buildings. "There's Camp Triumph. I'm going to put this baby down, and then I'll come around to help you out." His voice grew stern. "Don't get out before I come around. I don't want you hurt." He gave her a quick, expectant look.

"No, sir, I won't." There was that twinge of something good right in the center of her pelvis, and it rode up and down her vertebrae, giving her a bit of wiggle.

He nodded his satisfaction. "I'll check in on you to see if you're ready to go. I won't fly out without you." Chopper concentrated on maneuvering the large helicopter to make a soft landing.

Relieved she wouldn't have to hitch a ride back and risk missing her flight tomorrow, she asked, "How much time do we have?"

"I'm all yours until you're ready to go."

Felicity nodded. "Roger that. I appreciate it."

True to his word, Chopper landed softly, shut the enormous bird down, and ran around the front to help Felicity disembark. He gave her a pair of shades to keep the wind and debris out of her eyes. Felicity shivered with attraction when his fingers met hers. What a stupid, romantic notion to flash through her mind at a time like this. It was almost a physical spark, like static electricity. She really needed a decent guy and a good lay. She'd try to get that task taken care of as soon as she hit stateside.

Chopper pointed out the medical tent and ran with her through the flying dirt. Felicity entered the tent and was met with loud but ordered chaos. Anyone who didn't work in triage would have thought differently, but it was evident to Felicity that care was happening in the most efficient way possible.

She turned to hand her glasses back to the pilot, and the same reaction, tingling all over, starting at her fingers, happened again. Chopper's hand twitched, and he immediately shot a look in her direction, making it apparent to Felicity that their touch affected them both. After a cursory dusting off of her uniform, she went to work.

Ninety minutes later, she had stabilized every one of the injured except for one. Felicity began the last repair. She had to repair an arm at risk of being lost because of a lack of blood flow. She prepared to operate despite the complaints from the head medic that it wasn't worth the time since, in his opinion, it would not save the limb. They had been arguing for nearly five minutes, and Felicity had more than enough.

"Out here, Ma'am, we have to do what we can and not spend time and resources we don't have on those not likely to get any benefit. You wouldn't know that not working the field like us."

Felicity continued to set up a tray with the instruments she needed. "Bullshit. I have taken care of everyone else with high triage needs, and you assisted as needed. No one is at risk for loss of life or limb except this soldier, and I'll be damned if you stop me from trying to save his arm. Now back off and stand down."

"Major, that is a waste of time. I don't authorize the surgery."

"I have no intention of leaving this man with an assured limb loss. Why would you fight me on this?"

"I said, no, I do not authorize the surgery, and it is my field clinic."

A booming voice broke through the air that sizzled with discontent. "Doc, you have a problem I need to sort out so you can do your job?"

She turned to Chopper, standing there, his bulky arms folded the best they could and his legs spread wide. He was a blonde god like she imagined a young Odin of Norse fame to look. All movement stopped, and the room became completely silent.

"No thanks, Chopper, I have this." She turned to the medic. "For whom would my efforts be a waste of time, Sergeant, for whom?" She scrubbed.

"You're going to put this man in more danger, and for what, your pride?"

"Lieutenant, stand down." Chopper's voice was almost threatening. "Doc here is a Major and a physician, neither of which you are."

The sergeant turned away from the officers. Felicity spoke as she monitored the prepping of the patient and watched quietly as the man went under anesthesia.

"I'll ignore what you just said as one of those 'in the heat of battle' responses, but you let me be the judge of what is in this patient's best interest. His limb is not disposable. Having one or two arms makes the difference between surviving this shit with his dignity and body intact. Lord knows he will have enough to get through without his loss of a vital part of his physical self as well." Felicity turned to begin the prep of her patient and looked back at the Medic. "This patient has signed his agreement after both of us have fully disclosed. You can assist me or step away, but whatever you do, do it now."

The corpsman standing next to Felicity said, "I'll scrub up, Major."

"Thank you, Ramsey."

Without another word, Felicity scrubbed up and immediately worked on the arm, ignoring Chopper and the sergeant. Thankfully, it looked worse than it was, and she attached the few tendons and ligaments that were severed by the IUD fragment. Then reattaching the largest of the damaged veins and repairing the most significant tear of the muscle until she was satisfied she had done the best she could do.

She checked the pulse, and while it wasn't strong, it existed where none existed before. Now all they could hope for is that it was enough to keep the blood flow to the limb until a specialist could finish the operation.

The medical technician was washing up when he turned and said, "That was an amazing job, Ma'am."

"Well, I hope our efforts will do the trick, but always know, if we hadn't tried, it was a lost cause for sure. Let's get him set for transfer and the other two that need hospitalization. The rest, with some pain meds, should be able to make the drive.

"Yes, ma'am."

"Hey," she pulled out her phone, "before you do that, type your name on my notes. I'll put in a good word for you with the Colonel."

The tech grinned. "Yes, ma'am. Thank you, ma'am."

Felicity nodded. "Where can I grab a cup of coffee before I find Chopper?"

The tech pointed west. "The mess tent is that way, Ma'am."

As she walked into the mess tent, she could see her pilot drinking coffee and having dinner in the corner. When she headed for the coffee, a deep, mellow voice from behind her spoke close to her ear.

"Get something to eat. The mess will be closed when we get back, and you'll need something after that long session of work. Carbs and protein are what you need."

Chills ran down her arms, and her belly tingled. He didn't startle her. She actually relaxed when she recognized his voice. He spoke as if he cared, as if she meant something. It felt good. She wondered what it would be like if he were hers to lay claim to.

"You know, I could have handled things back there. I'm used to running the show in the world."

"Well, guess someone thought differently. One corpsman came to find me and said, you might appreciate my presence. Guess he was wrong."

"No, well, I appreciated the gesture, but not the interference itself. I can hold my own, Chopper."

"Damn right, you can. Once I got there, I saw you had it all under control, but I had to make sure. Couldn't have the Doc I brought in mistreated, now could I?" His voice held something akin to appreciation and protectiveness that surprised her.

"What's your name?" she asked as she continued pouring coffee.

"What?" he asked.

"Not Chopper, your actual name."

"I'm only known as Chopper. Even if I told you, I don't think I would even answer to it anymore." He nodded in the direction of the food. "The beef is pretty good. I'm going to check on the helicopter and supervise the wounded onboarding. Eat, hit the head, and then come on out to the bird. We should be ready for you."

"Oh, but I should supervise the patients."

"Major, do you remember my two rules?"

Felicity frowned. "Yes, but we are on land right now."

His voice lowered for her ears only. "But, sweetheart, you're going to need a ride home." He wasn't wrong, damn him.

"You are entirely too bossy, Major." She stared at him, body tensely held, but after a few seconds, her shoulders relaxed. "Fine, you're right. I am tired and hungry, but what about your dinner?"

He grinned. "It's my second helping. I'm more than full."

Felicity smiled back and shook her head. She could only imagine how much food it took to fill up this guy. She was a decent height at 5 foot 9 inches, but his additional six or seven inches and his build belied delicate portions.

"I'll finish up here and be out shortly."

"I figure you got about fifteen minutes, so eat. We have to take the little, seemingly insignificant moments when we can because life holds no guarantees. The military knows that better than most."

There he was, bossing her again. Felicity nodded, and Chopper grinned again before his long, muscular legs took him out of the mess tent. She must really be tired because he looked mighty nice, and she never looked at the men around her as potential dates. Never date your workmates, she reminded herself. Been there, done that, trashed the tee shirt. Felicity nodded at the server and told him what she wanted.

The flight back to the post was quiet as Felicity monitored the three patients who slept relatively comfortably all the way. As the last stretcher left the helicopter and the last patient's briefing complete allowing the technicians to take the patient inside, she turned to Chopper.

"Thanks for the ride and hanging out while I worked. If you hadn't, I'd have missed my transport back tomorrow."

"No problem, Major. May you have fair winds and following seas on your next duty station."

"Felicity, my name is Felicity Torrez, and if you ever are in Hood, look me up. You can always find me at the hospital or the clinics."

They shook hands, and Felicity turned to go when a light hand on her shoulder stopped her. She turned and glanced back. "Felicity, I like you. Anyone who calmly handled the situation you did today is definitely worth some time getting to know. Would you like to relax and listen to music? I know it's a crap pickup line, and I don't know if that is what this is, exactly, but I'd like to spend a little time with you before you leave tomorrow afternoon."

"How do you know I leave in the afternoon?"

He smiled and shrugged. "I'm a pilot. I know the standard flight schedules."

Felicity was a rule player. The rules said no mingling while on deployment, but she was about to leave, and just once, she wanted to live on the wild side. Break a rule. She looked up at Chopper and smiled back boldly. If that is where this led, then she would follow.

"Okay, sure, I'd like that."

Chopper's room was on the bottom floor next to a side door of the building used for barracks. "You're not in a tent?"

"I wouldn't have asked you back to a tent, Felicity. I mean, maybe to shoot the breeze or play cards or something, but not on your last night in country." His tone was just a hair chastising, and it didn't annoy her, which did bother her.

"I can only spend a few hours. Besides, I'm sure you have PT in the morning."

"I just got back from some fieldwork this morning and then that quick run with you this afternoon. I have forty-eight hours to sleep, eat, and play."

"And you don't want to fill your free time with me when I won't be here after tomorrow." She shrugged. "And I'm pretty boring."

"Sit down and tell me about yourself because I'm sure you aren't anything close to boring." He smiled. "But if you are, I'll let you know."

She smiled back. "Thanks."

Felicity could have told him even her parents thought she was, and that meant something, but she didn't. She sat and accepted the can of cold pop. She looked over to where he'd come from in the corner of the room and found that there was a refrigerator large enough for about twelve cans of pop but nothing else. In this heat, what else did you want?

"Pretty nifty you got this in your room." She held up her can. He grinned.

"It came with the room. I mean, obviously, whoever got it here couldn't take it home on the transport, so they left it, and I'm the lucky stiff who benefitted. Well, and my friends," he nodded in her direction, "which now includes you."

Chopper unlaced his boots and kicked them off. "Take yours off if you're more comfortable. I've just been in these suckers for two days now, and it's time to let the feet air. I throw foot powder in them but no telling how bad the stink might be."

Fascinated, she watched him slowly take off his desert boots and then smiled when his obvious pleasure was audible. "Better than sex," he said as he stretched his legs out slowly.

She laughed. "Good to know, but there are occasions where I'd be more inclined to have sex, no offense."

"None taken. Now, tell me about yourself. Start at the beginning. Where did you grow up?"

The next four hours were spent laughing and telling stories about their experiences. By the end of the evening, they were even teasing.

"I bet you are a subordinate's worst nightmare when you aren't happy," observed Felicity.

"You can count on that, and when I need to get something done, I can be a terror. But when things are going well, I am the life of the party. Just ask my sisters." Chopper defended himself.

"No, I bet they were ecstatic when you left home so they could date."

"Damn straight. I left them with strict instructions that no one was to accept a marriage proposal without my say-so." He spoke with pride.

"And have they?"

He looked horrified. "Of course not." Then he chuckled. "But they were so in love, I didn't have the heart to say anything but, good choice. However, to the men they chose, I said a few more private words."

"Oh, I bet you did." She wished someone cared enough about her making the right choice to want to meet her prospective man before marriage. She checked her watch. "It's late, and I have to go. Thank you so much for a really great evening."

"Felicity, I want to look you up when we get back stateside. We rotate back from this unit we are attached to in about a month."

"Give me your phone." She entered her phone number in the cell and sent herself a message. "There, you have my number." He stood as she stood.

"Thanks." He stood closer. "Can I kiss you goodnight? I'm saying that here because, while I intend on walking you to your side of the base, I don't think publicly kissing is a good idea. We don't know who is watching."

"I agree," she said a little breathlessly. She hardly noticed as Chopper got even closer.

"Felicity? Is it okay?" He was so close that his breath anointed her cheek with warmth, and his mere presence had her pulses racing.

"I-I yes, it's okay if you kiss me. I'm not very good but—"

His lips lightly grazed hers in short bursts of sweetness, touching her lips in the center and both sides before settling on a true melding of needs. His tongue found its way inside her mouth as he explored her inner recesses. She met the intruding organ with hers, dueling, tangling, and stroking each other.

She pulled back because of her lack of adequate oxygen. Felicity placed her head on his chest as she tried to control her raspy, ragged breaths.

"Beautiful. I won't forget that kiss as long as I live. I won't forget you, Felicity Torrez."

Her libido caused her inner core muscles to seize as if to cramp with the response. It was indeed painful, and she realized it must be a little of what men felt when their libido was skyrocketing. She didn't go for blondes, usually, but this man pushed all the right buttons. And she needed to get out of here. She may have thought she was up to the one-night stand, and something told her he might take her up on it if she asked right now, but that isn't what she wanted for her life. She needed more and wouldn't take anything less.

She raised her head as he lifted her chin to meet his eyes. "Let's get you home. I'll be calling you once I arrive back. While we are over here, I'm usually in the field, so saying I will call or answer one would be a lie. But like I said, I have about a month, and then I'll call you. That alright?"

"Of course. I'll be busy as well, so no worries on that score." She sighed and stepped back. "I need to go."

He leaned down and slipped on his sneakers before wrapping his arm around her as he led her to the door. She turned to him. "Chopper, I don't think you should take me back. I'll walk in the light, and it's only about five minutes."

"No, I'll walk back with you. I won't touch you, and neither will anyone else, although it may damn well kill me."

She chuckled with a touch of melancholy. "I know, so it would be easier if I do it this way."

"I'll see you back, Felicity, and that's all I'm saying on the subject. Let's go."

"You're so bossy," she said as they walked outside in the arid, still too warm night.

"I know, you told me. But I take care of all who belong to my family, which includes close friends. You are part of my group now."

She didn't know what to say since she was leaving tomorrow. She had been in this too hot, too lonely place for six months and when she finally found someone she might really like, she had to leave. She might have been on the fence about it before, but now she was sure. Time to get out. Felicity had been part of the Army for fourteen plus years. Almost eleven in the Army and four in military residency.

"I can be your friend." She wanted more, but if all he was offering was friendship, she'd have to be satisfied with it. They might never cross paths again, anyway.

He gave her a strange look, as though he had something to say but didn't. Instead, he said as she was turning away, "It's Darrell. Darrell Frazier and I look forward to our next meeting, Felicity Torrez. I'll take you to dinner, and we can discuss the merits of having an overnighter."

Felicity smiled, knowing it was just talk. "Goodbye, Darrell Frazier. It's been nice getting to know you."

"See you later, sweetheart."

Chapter 1

Two years later

Chopper, once again, looked at the papers that told him he had retired from the United States Marine Corps. He'd served in the Army, Navy, and Marine Corps at one time or another assigned to Zed's SEAL team, which is how he met Zayden Wellesley and Ryder Mason. River Bennett was on Special Ops teams with Chopper in the Army.

Chopper had piloted with the Army Deltas, then moved to the Navy SEAL teams,¹ but they had plenty of pilots, so he finished his couple of stints with them, moving to "the few, the proud, the Marines" and ended his career with the Night Stalkers. It was a wild, patchwork way to make one's career, but other than telling him he was crazy, Chopper was allowed the shift. He was one of the best in his extractions and tactical moves. Everyone had wanted him. He always brought his team home, even though it was hairy at times but at a tremendous personal price.

The adventure had been an enormous adrenalin rush, but now he was looking for something else. He wanted a family, roots, build a forever, and the first person who came to mind was Felicity Torrez, M.D. The woman was never too far from his mind since he found her standing her ground in a medical tent in the field. She was feisty and knew her stuff. She'd saved that soldier's arm, and his gut burned needy when he thought of her.

He had tried to find her nearly six months later, but she had already left the service. He had gotten stuck in other parts of the world doing his thing, and when he got back to the states, she had changed her phone number and melted into the civilian world. It took him another year to find someone who had an idea of where Felicity was from, except that information wouldn't help because Felicity had said her family moved to somewhere in Oregon. He simply didn't know where. He'd thought to try all the Torrez families in the area, but there were too many, so no luck there.

He'd called around as he was getting ready to ETS and was given some ideas of places military doctors might go to work. But there was a big world out there, and after he called local hospitals to her hometown, He was about to give up. He couldn't find where she had gone until, by accident, he heard a former Army doctor was running a village clinic.

Hoping it was Felicity, he'd stopped and seen a buddy of his who was now running a training program in Southeast Alaska on a small island. SEAL Commander, oops now Captain, Zayden (Zed) Wellesley had asked Chopper to sign on as his pilot for the times they would need him to do drops and extractions in training, but Chopper couldn't until he followed that vague lead further north. If he had a chance to find Felicity, he wanted to. He hadn't been able to get her out of his mind, and he wasn't a man to give up easily.

He spent several months flying for a small outfit that always needed more pilots in the summer months. As the fall progressed, the flights were less frequent, and his services weren't needed again until the late spring. He'd hit every community he could anyway and no Felicity. After speaking to or visiting every clinic with a doctor, of which there weren't many, Chopper decided it was time to regroup. Maybe he'd ask Zed's computer whiz kid to see what he could find.

He'd gotten back just in time to help locate Alesha, Zed's now pregnant wife, and their kids in the avalanche. He signed on with Zed's multi-service, multi-agency training center, but he needed to do more, so he hired out to a few other flight outfits and used their planes and helicopters most of the time. Chopper still felt restless, but time would help him settle in that and a schedule. The icing on the cake would be to find Felicity Torrez and see where that would lead him.

He looked out his front window and grumbled at the weather. Today, the rain wouldn't stop. Where were the beautiful days of his last trip to the lush green paradise of this Alaskan island? He chuckled to himself. He wouldn't put it past his friend and former teammate to have staged it for his benefit.

He could hear Zed joke, "What's a little subterfuge amongst brothers?"

Well, he could unpack another few boxes, but something told him it wasn't time to do that just yet. His gut was smarter than he was, so he replaced his important papers in the fireproof container in the box marked, of course, *Important Papers* and headed to his truck.

Chopper had returned to Southeast Alaska to explore the options now available to him. Looking around on his fourth month as a civilian pilot made him scratch his head in second thoughts. The income was decent, but it would be much better if he ran his own flight business. But he was looking to set up forever, and he needed a woman he loved to do that. No, the flight company would have to wait until he knew where that forever home would be.

Felicity Torrez, without trying at all, had gotten under his skin like no woman ever had. Chopper had dates and one-night stands. No one could call him a monk but never had one stuck it out through more than a few missions. Now he wanted a family, which meant staying in one place, coming home most evenings, and one woman. All things he'd never had before. And he wanted them with Felicity. Or at least he wanted to see if he did.

Zed was his career-long buddy, and with his new assignment on the small base on Quartz Island, the side jobs, and now the search and rescue team he'd joined, it looked and sounded like an excellent springboard to civilian life. And maybe Zed had some ideas about Felicity, too. His wife was a nurse, and Alaska was a low population state.

Rainforest was not an exaggeration, however. Even a temperate one was wet eighty percent of the time. Flights were often canceled now that it was one of two rainy seasons. Fuck, he was going to grow webbed feet soon. Time to go and see what he could do to fill his day.

Chopper walked into the operations office and rapped on Captain Zayden Wellesley's door. "The Captain won't see you without an appointment."

Chopper turned to eyeball the twenty-something-year-old young man sitting in the Gunny's chair. "Are you the clerk?"

"I'm Corporal Jamison. Who are you, and why are you here? More to the question, how did you get in here?"

"You must be new," stated Chopper without answering the Corporal's rudely presented questions. "I know all the Captain's staff but have never met you."

Frustrated, the clerk buzzed into Zed's office. "Sir, there is a Mr. Chopper out here to see you. If you want me to—"

"Oh, great, send him in."

"But, sir, your meeting is on the schedule for—"

"Thank you, Jamison, I know what time my meeting is. Send Lt. Colonel Frazier in, please." Zed's voice held a hint of frustration.

The clerk replaced the phone displaying his own touch of temper as he did. "You may..." Chopper had already opened the door. "Well, then go right on in, sir."

Chopper looked back with a stare he reserved for rude, officer-chasing women, out-of-control children, and out-of-line subordinates. The stern look could shrivel the most caustic person. "Thank you, Corporal." Chopper closed the door behind him and sent a grin in his friend's direction. "You know I'm retired."

Zed shrugged. "You retired as a Light Colonel. I didn't lie. But I still beat you."

"Yeah, Ryder helped you out, you old dog."

"Nah, I earned this position. Ryder just let me know a few days before anyone else knew it was coming down the pike. Besides, I didn't jump services."

"Yes, but I have friends everywhere," said Chopper smugly as he sat in one of the chairs in front of Zed's desk.

Zed laughed and leaned back in his chair. "I'm making new ones every training session."

Chopper settled in his seat and nodded. "Okay, you win this round. How's the family?"

Zed raised an eyebrow. "Good, but they're all upset with you. Alli said that you haven't stopped by since the snow slide." He put his hand up. "Don't say it. She absolutely refuses to call the hiking incident an avalanche, and I humor her. She's been sick a lot with this new recruit she's creating. She wanted me to call you this weekend and guilt you into coming. I thought we'd barbeque. Whatcha think? You free?"

Chopper hesitated before answering. His expression became pensive. "Maybe. I know I haven't been by since the accident, but that wasn't long ago."

"Yeah, I know, but Alli is three months pregnant now, and she hasn't been queasy in almost a week. It's something worth celebrating. Besides, this training group leaves on Sunday. So, Saturday?"

"Yeah, Saturday. I'll bring the beer."

"Good, because I can't buy any alcohol until Alli delivers. Then she'll be nursing, so likely not then either."

"Yeah, man, TMI. I'll be on beer call until you can buy your own."

Zed nodded and stared at his friend. His expression was now serious. "Appreciate it. Now, why are you here? As annoying as Jamison is, he's right. I do have a meeting in less than ten minutes."

"Right. I wondered if I could use your whiz kid to try to find a prior service member I met in Afghanistan a couple of years before I retired. She was an Army doctor who said she was getting out soon." Zed nodded but didn't interrupt him. Chopper wished he would say something. He continued. "Anyway, I contacted River Bennett, but he was about to go window shopping in South America and said he'd be back soon. Before I contacted him again, I wondered if you could see if you could find her."

Zed reached for a pen and paper. "What's her name?"

"In the Army, she was Major Felicity Torrez, M.D. She was traced to an agency in Denver that did locums, and it was thought she was up North. That was a bust. Do you think you could find her for me?"

"She's special." It wasn't a question.

"She is."

"I'll get on this. Alli might have heard of her since she's a nurse that seems to be friends with everyone in this whole damn state."

"Yeah, sometimes rank doesn't mean a fucking thing."

"You got that right. Okay, I have to check into the meeting. I'll let you know what I find out on Saturday. Come anytime but by five."

"I'm doing a couple of runs to neighboring islands Saturday, so likely to be late afternoon around four."

"Sounds good. See you then."

The men shook hands, and the phone rang before Chopper had closed the door. Chopper said in his no-nonsense voice. "The Captain needs coffee and a snack."

"Yes, sir." Jamison nodded, checked the phone, and briskly rose from his desk and walked into another room. Chopper smiled as he left the building. The kid was too easy to mess with. Zed would appreciate the snack, though.

Chapter 2

F elicity pushed her calendar and computer further in front of her. She hated
staring at the same names over and over, but that was part of the job. High-
risk patients non-compliant with medications and engaged in non-compliant
lifestyles were the only preloaded descriptions listed. She had changed the
wording on some records, but the standardized computer program she was re-
quired to use did not have an explanation that adequately addressed what she
most often faced here in the Alaskan bush.

It wasn't apathy or noncompliance in the way the program meant. It was a
reliance on natural medications that families had used for generations. It was
a learned distrust of most professions and, in her case, the medications she
brought with her. In addition to the stoic Native People, it was non-native local
people, many having left the lower forty-eight for Alaska's islands and bushland
to live a life away from prying eyes. These off-the-grid residents blended well into some of the Alaska Native elders' desire to live with as little intervention as
possible.

Felicity had been hired by the Indian Health Services through the Defense
Health Agency Civilian Corps to meet the medical and often mental health
needs of their Native people. She treated the non-native people in the area due
to a high-needs rural federal grant, and she was a provider for the Veterans Ad-
ministration. Alaska had a high number of veterans.

Native and non-natives lived a unique existence in their own small communities that corporate America did not understand. She tried to integrate and
build trust where she was able. It took patience and sometimes just plain luck.
She was appeasing people on both sides of the practice, and it could be exhausting on some days.

Felicity had undergone cultural awareness training for a week to cover
those unique needs. It wasn't nearly enough. She scheduled another training for

local homeopathic and herbal medicines in the area so she could learn more. Other providers interested in meeting the needs of their patients were going to attend, and Felicity was excited.

Alaskans were a hardy breed. It was often said that the British had the attitude of the stiff upper lip, pressing on in adverse times, and she thought it was true, but Felicity had worked alongside many troops from other countries during her time in the service, and while they all showed a tremendous amount of determination, she had no doubt Alaskans beat many people in stoicism and sheer determination by a mountain man's mile.

She was here to gain experience, test the waters to see if this was the kind of work she'd like to do and pay off her recently acquired student loans. She took a few college classes on Native Medicines, Alaskan Culture and Alaskan Anthropology. The army did a great job eliminating any college debt, but Felicity had a little more incurred with her extra training once she left the military. It was a different life, for sure.

The government paid off her current loans in the first year, and in exchange, she agreed to work in vulnerable, high-needs areas. Thankfully, her loans were paid now, but she had one more year of contracted service, giving her the option to change directions if she wanted to at the end of the time, but she was beginning to absolutely love Alaska. The lifestyle was easy. The people were laid back. And she had met some military here that she clicked with.

In fact, Alesha Wellesley had just sent her a text to invite her to a cookout at their house this weekend. Evidently, there would be current and former military and a few locals and alphabet agency people in attendance. If Felicity stayed in Alaska, she would need to decide if she stayed with the DHA or hung her own shingle.

If she went solo, she would want Alli as her nurse. Alli's husband, Captain Zed Wellesley, a Navy SEAL now trainer, was a force to be reckoned with according to all reports, but his wife and children seemed oblivious to his bluster. Alli laughed at that description.

"Zed is a confident man that turns into a hard ass at work and a softie at home once the uniform is off. Just wait until you meet him. You'll see."

"Soft? Most service members are hard noses by the time they get to the rank of 0-6."

"It's true, and he can be, but I promise I can get whatever I want if I frame it right."

Felicity joined in her friend's laughter. "I'll take your word for it."

Felicity thought about how she wanted what Alli had now that Felicity had completed her obligations elsewhere. She'd stayed in until she hit her ten-year mark and then transferred that officer pension from the Army to her current employer. Now she was beginning to feel established in her little town, and her pension was growing.

She grabbed the afternoon floatplane back to Port Refuge, thought about the man she had met on her last night in-country, and sighed. Chopper, no, Darrell. She had thought he was full of his own importance for a few short minutes but soon realized he was knowledgeable and compassionate. Almost protective. And bossy, she remembered with a wry smile.

She enjoyed talking with Chopper, sharing part of herself as he shared some of himself. He was a different type of man. When he demanded she eat something, it wasn't because his rank meant he could. It was because he was concerned for her. That was something she had rarely had in her adult life outside of her parents. Her brothers were happy she was doing what she wanted, but they had their own lives.

"I'm looking for something else," she'd told him.

"I hear you. Something that isn't so regimented." He nodded as she continued.

"I'm an organized person, myself, and I like schedules and consistency, but it's time for me to step out on my own. Not follow along behind the leader. I need to lead, even if it's just me."

"I understand. So where do you plan to start out?"

"Maybe I transition to the DHA Civilian Corps and decide from there or go as a private provider in a military hospital. I'd be a civilian worker, and yet the middle ground might do it for me for a little while. I want to settle down, and maybe I'll find the right place if I pick an area and work there for a while."

"Sounds like you've got a plan. Do you mind if I look you up when I retire in a few years? I'm at retirement now, so when my commitment time is up for making this last rank, I'm toying with the idea of going out into the world and spreading my wings there."

"I'd like that."

That is what she did, but she wondered what Chopper or Darrell, as he finally told her, had ultimately done. While working in the military, she often found herself in the roughest areas of those deployed. At home, she learned Alaska wasn't just a part of the U. S. they were their own world in many ways.

Felicity was glad she had taken the transition when she was so burned out with the military. It allowed her to be more tolerant of being ignored, pushed off, or downright refused because she wasn't local. It was a new challenge she'd so desperately needed at the time. From what she could gather, that "local" moniker might take a while to gain. Two years was nowhere near enough time. Maybe two decades would be more like it.

The temperate rainforest, the antithesis of the Middle East, was much preferred to the drought and desert as she watched them approach the inlet for landing. This little island was a wet paradise in its own way. Thinking of heading over to Alli's tomorrow, Felicity gathered her things from the seat and waited until she was assisted onto the dock, then waited on her suitcase and medical bag to be unloaded before heading to grab a quick dinner on her way home as per her routine.

The following day, the sun was trying desperately to make an appearance. The jury was still out whether it was strong enough today to win that battle. As she ate a breakfast burrito and drank her coffee, Felicity read her appointment calendar. It was like living in two different worlds.

On the one hand, the villages and bush communities often had very few amenities and modern conveniences, but when she was back on Cache Island in her small community of Eagle's Landing, she had all she wanted and more. It was the larger of the two towns on the island, with nearly ten thousand now. More when the tourists were here, and the military were doing their maneuvers on Quarts Island. Zed, Alli's husband, ran an elitist training center.

There was another, smaller community on the island called Port Refuge, and her office, as well as Alli's home, was located there. Close to Alli's place was River Bennett and his fiancée Kayla Rhea's enormous property. River was prior Army from Zed's earlier days, and there just wasn't any other way to say it, but while he was down to earth and a generally nice guy, he was bossy like Zed. He did love Kayla with all his heart, and that was easy to see. Felicity sighed. She wanted that.

Again, Chopper's face, alight with that mischievous grin, popped into her mind's eye, and Felicity thought about what had intrigued her. What had drawn her to him? His honesty, candidness and his confidence. Oh, and his protectiveness. She had never been attracted to a man who was the "what do you want to do" type. Darrell was not that guy at all. He would decide and then make sure it was alright with you but not wait on his date to figure out the evening's plan.

She liked a choice, but when the situation called for it, Felicity wanted a man who tactically assessed the situation and then chose his path, walking it with confidence. Chopper would be that man. Felicity sighed again. She seemed to be doing that a lot lately. Felicity wished she could locate Chopper right now, but when her phone was stolen as she was preparing to ETS and then had to change phone services anyway, she lost only one number she had hoped to retain, his. Time to find her keys and get to the office. Maybe on Saturday, she could get Zed to help her find him.

"WHO IS ON CALL FOR the practice this weekend?" asked Janis Svendsen.

Felicity checked their calendar. Janis and Jans Svendsen were a couple who had been at the clinic for six months. Both were doctors who were competent and easy to work with. They were building a friendly rapport with the community, but Felicity could already tell they would not stay past their contract. It was too different from their Minnesota home with its seclusion and lack of city amenities.

"The Blaine Clinic. Then it's your week to go to the island."

"Yep, I'm leaving early Monday so I can get back Friday morning."

"I hadn't expected to get back as early as I did, but everyone was healthy, and I had few follow-ups other than the usuals."

"I hope that continues."

The hospital took care of all acute needs during the weekend and evenings. Their clinic and three others each took a weekend a month, so Felicity only had to cover 4 nights a year. It was a sweet deal, really, but providers came and went too often to build a solid friendship. Even though Felicity had been here for only a year and a half, she was the old-timer with few exceptions.

Patients deserved better than that, so it would be a real commitment if she were to stay. Felicity just needed someone to balance her life out. Maybe she would meet someone at Alli's tomorrow afternoon. If she did, she would wait on trying to find Chopper.

Another thing she had taken some time to get used to was the long summer daylight hours. This would be her second summer, and she still hesitated when Alli said they started gathering around five. It would be another six hours before the sun lowered enough to need lights outside.

Alli and Zed had a nice place in a sweet circle of three houses. Felicity didn't know who lived in the third home, but Alli lived on that circle as a child and still did when her parents moved South. When Alli met and then married Zed, they sold her family's home to the military for trainee housing.

They had invited felicity to go boating with them from their newly refurbished dock, but she caught a virus and had to stay home. That was last summer. She hoped they would invite her again sometime. Alli said Zed was overprotective, so it might not be this summer while she was pregnant. Smiling ruefully at the conversation, Felicity gathered the items to make her Froggie-Eye salad.

The following morning flew by like most Saturday mornings. Felicity did her weekly house cleaning, laundry and grocery shopping by noon. She hadn't wanted to eat much, so she had a little soup for lunch. Alli had said they had too much food already when Felicity insisted on bringing something. She would finally meet Alesha's husband.

Felicity was anxious. Not sure why but never one to ignore her inner signals, she took care to apply a light touch of makeup and styled her long hair into soft waves. It was the longest it had been in well over a decade. Satisfied, she grabbed her salad, her keys, a hoodie and her bag before she left, ready to have some fun.

CHOPPER CLIMBED INTO the helicopter for the last time. He was tired. The job he'd taken on to help the construction crew had been more labor intensive than he'd expected, and he hadn't been able to take much of a break. The supplies he'd hauled over didn't fit where they had wanted it, and he was expected to wait until they cleared a larger spot.

Then he'd needed to make two additional trips more than the three he had contracted for. He recommended a barge next time to bring it all over by water, but the foreman just laughed as though Chopper was making a joke. He checked his bird and glanced at the time. Damn, it was almost five. Good thing he'd dropped off the beer before he left so Zed could ice it. He'd land on the helipad at Zed's place to save time.

"HELLO, WELLESLEY'S residence."

That voice was slightly familiar, but she was sure it wasn't River's, and she didn't really know any of Alli and Zed's friends. A loud round of laughter could be heard through the line, making hearing the other person difficult. "Hi, sounds like the party started without me. Is Zed around?"

"Yes and no. Is it an emergency? It might be easier if I took a message. Oh, wait, here he comes." Felicity handed to phone to Zed and walked back to get the ice she had originally come in to grab.

Just as she took a bite of the perfectly grilled halibut on her plate, a loud helicopter landed behind them. Felicity sent an inquiring look in Alli's direction. Alli smiled in return and waved her closer.

"This is Zed's good friend. They served together, and then when Zed came here, and Chopper went North."

"Chopper?" Lots of pilots probably went by that handle, right?

"Yes. Odd name, but since he mostly flies helicopters, I guess that's where his nickname came from. Boys and their toys."

Alli smiled again and walked toward the small group surrounding a blonde man as tall as Zed sporting mirrored sunglasses. Felicity's heart pounded. What were the odds that Zed's long-time friend was her Chopper? Not high, surely. And yet...

Felicity watched from a distance until Zed and Alli returned to the gathering, and flyboy went into the house through the backdoor. She went back to eating her dinner and talking to some of the graduates of Zed's most recent class, all the while keeping her radar tuned to Chopper's voice.

They were an interesting and diverse group, and Felicity found herself engrossed in some of their stories. It felt good to mingle in a group of similarly minded people speaking about things she was familiar with. She set down her plate and reached for her drink when she heard her name.

A hand touched her shoulder. Felicity turned as Alli spoke. "Sorry to inter-rupt, but I wanted to introduce one of my favorite doctors to—"

"Felicity."

"Darrell? It is you. I—" Chopper's lips came crashing down on hers in a thirsty kiss. Without thought, she kissed him back, equally parched.

Chapter 3

"Um... well, I guess you know each other, then," said Alli awkwardly. Zed came up and slapped Chopper on the back. "I forgot to tell Alli about locating your girl, but I guess this is the Felicity you have been looking for? It never dawned on me you might have been looking for Doc until now. Sorry man, you could have found her two days ago."

"If I hadn't tried to do it all on my own, I could have found her months ago," replied a frustrated Chopper, his eyes never leaving hers.

"Yeah, well, better late than never," said Zed. "Grab some eats, and you two go into the den to talk. I don't imagine you need an audience for this reunion."

"FELICITY?" CHOPPER asked her hoping she would agree.

He didn't know what had come over him when he saw her, but he didn't think she was opposed to his greeting, given how easily she returned his kiss.

"Um, yeah, that's good. I'd like that."

Felicity licked her lips and only then dropped her gaze, and he grew hard thinking of what else she could lick. He wanted to go for round two, but he instinctively knew that would be pushing it. Neither of them were young kids, and he and his libido needed to remember that.

Chopper smiled. "Good. I'm starving and dry as the desert." His hand naturally slid into place against the small of Felicity's back as he lightly steered her toward the food.

Once inside, Chopper was right at home, having been in this same room with Zed many times.

"Eat. We'll talk afterward," encouraged Felicity.

Chopper nodded. "Tell me what you've done since leaving the Army. Tell me what brought you here while I eat?"

Chopper listened intently as Felicity filled in about her decision to transition into civilian life. Her training for preparation to come to Alaska, her restless time off, and ultimately accepting a position in Southeast Alaska. By then, she'd covered the first six months post-deployment, and Chopper had polished off his dinner, one glass of tea, and had opened a beer.

"Sure you don't want one?" He held up his can.

"I don't drink beer." She gave a mock shudder. "But I do like wine." She raised her plastic glass of wine. "Now, tell me why you're here."

"First Zed, then you. He offered me a job before I got out, but I couldn't think about staying in one place until I had looked for you. I started to search for you at your last duty station, but only a few were still there. Your phone number changed, and I refused to believe that you had done that on purpose, but I had to acknowledge it was possible."

She shook her head. "Nope. My phone was stolen, and then that service provider doesn't work on the island, so I traded companies. I couldn't retrieve my numbers."

"Well, luckily, your old colonel was still around, and he told me what he knew."

"That couldn't have been much because we weren't the best co-workers."

"No, but he did point me in the direction of where he'd gotten a referral request from and to a friend, Martha Roberts. I went from there."

"You did a good job locating me."

"It wasn't easy. You are one hard woman to find. I was up North for months trying to locate you. It never dawned on me you would be in the Southeast. When I thought village, I thought north."

"Yes, many do, but as you have learned since being here, they are all over the state." She paused. "You really spent time looking for me?" her look of disbelief was exchanged for awe.

He leaned forward and touched her cheek. "I did. Obviously, unsuccessfully, but we're here now, nonetheless."

Felicity smiled and laid her hand over his for a moment before leaning back into the sofa. "A little providence never hurt."

Chopper nodded and leaned back himself. "True. If I had just given out a little more information, I would have found you months ago."

She gave him a mischievous grin. "All you would have had to do was type my name in the National Provider Records, and I would have come up. It would have told you where to find me."

"The hell you say. Well, fate stepped in so I wouldn't have to be crawling around in the dark anymore. Wonder why no one told me that?"

"Maybe they didn't believe you or was trying to keep me hidden if that is what I wanted. You do look rough with that long hair and your scruffy beard. Besides, the locals tend to keep things to themselves."

His hand came up and rubbed his face. "Yeah, I've let things go a little. But damn, I'm glad we finally connected."

"Me too." Felicity appeared suddenly shy, and he needed her to talk, not stall on him.

"I've got so many questions."

"Really? Well, fire away," said Felicity. That perked her up. Good.

Several hours had gone by when Katrina, Zed's eldest, came into the room. "Uncle Chopper, daddy says time to mingle. Besides, he needs help with the fireworks."

Chopper laughed. "Tell him we're coming. I wouldn't want him to burn down the house."

Katrina planted her hands on her hips. "Daddy would never do that."

Chopper grinned and agreed. "No, I'm only teasing Kitkat."

"I am too old for silly nicknames, Uncle Chopper." Her prim demeanor had him sober as best he could.

"Of course. I'll try to remember that." And with an elaborate flounce, she left the room.

Chopper and Felicity chuckled once the pre-teen disappeared around the corner. "That kid is a card," said Chopper. "And so grown up. She has been since she was five and telling everyone what to do. When her mom passed, things got hard, but as you can see, she is her father's daughter."

"Yes, Alli has told me a lot of the story."

"Right, I'm going to kiss you again, Felicity. Once is not enough."

"Oh, I get a choice this time?" she asked with her right brow arched in mock chastisement.

Chopper appeared duly repentant. "About that, I'm sorry. It's just that finally seeing you again after looking for so long," he shrugged and looked sheepishly in her direction.

"Are you going to talk, or are you going to kiss me before someone else comes searching for you again?"

"I'm kissing." His lips came down softer but no less urgent. He stepped closer to Felicity as she leaned in the last few inches to close the gap. His fingers were tangled in her long trellises, and he could feel her hand slide up the back of his neck. Tongues sought each other and together explored the depths, tangling and jabbing until finally, they had to part for survival.

Breathing hard, Felicity panted her next words. "I think I need the bathroom to pull myself together. That was some kiss."

"I need a cold shower, but I won't get it. Go to the bathroom, and I'll try to settle things down."

Chopper picked up their garbage and swung by the kitchen to dump them before Felicity returned, and he took her hand. He half expected her to pull back, but she didn't. That was encouraging. When they arrived where Zed was assembling the fireworks, Chopper turned to Felicity and nodded to Alli, who had walked closer to the couple.

"I'll be back when we're done." His look turned serious. "I'm not finished with you tonight, woman." He looked over at Alli. "Don't let her leave before I get through here."

"I can't hogtie her, Chopper."

"Felicity, I need your word." He hoped he communicated how sincere he was.

"You have it. I won't leave until you come back."

Chopper nodded and dropped a light peck on her deep red lips, and he walked away, whistling as he went. Felicity's gaze followed the blonde Adonis to the Wellesley boat and watched it pull out into the water a short way. The partygoers and the surrounding neighbors would be able to see the display safely.

Alli turned to Felicity. "Oh. My. God. You have a lot of blanks to fill in, girl, but I'm the hostess. It will have to be later, but not much later."

Felicity laughed. "I'm not sure I can fill in all the blanks because I still have a few. But I promise we'll talk."

The fireworks went off without a hitch, and the children labeled Zed and Chopper heroes, but Felicity was getting as tired as the children who were being bundled up and taken home. Alli began gathering her brood as well.

"These little guys need to crawl into their beds. It's eleven o'clock. I can't believe they lasted as long as they did. Do you want to come in with me while I take care of them?" Alli finished her invitation with a yawn she quickly tried to cover.

"No, it looks like you are as tired as the children and to be honest, I'm feeling the call of my sheets as well. Do you think the guys will be back soon?"

"Yes. Zed will say goodnight to the stragglers and do some cleanup, and I'll go on to bed soon, but I'm sure you won't have to wait long for your man."

"Stop. He isn't my man. I just... never mind. I'll talk to you tomorrow."

Arms slid around her waist from behind, and Felicity instinctively leaned back into those solid and comforting arms. A gravelly voice spoke low and sweet in her ear. "I might not be your man right now, sweetheart, but I want to be. And if my instincts aren't wrong, you would like that too."

"Maybe," she said, ending with a yawn she quickly covered as she tried to pull out of his hold. He didn't allow it. "Oh, sorry. That was rude of me."

"Nope, you're tired, and so am I. I'm going to take one of Zed's cars home and bring it back in the morning. Let me give you a ride home. I don't like you driving when you're this tired. It isn't safe."

"But I'm safe. No, I try to go nowhere on Sundays and just relax at home. I'll be fine."

"Next time, we can come in one vehicle, and this won't happen."

"I like bringing my own car so that I can leave whenever I want. Which, tonight is now."

"Hold on. I'll grab the keys from the house and can follow you." Felicity started to speak, but Darrell interrupted. "Let me do this, Felicity. I need to know you're safely home."

She hesitated and then smiled. "Thank you. I'll get in my car and wait for you but hurry. I really am fading fast."

He dropped a spontaneous kiss on her unsuspecting lips. "Be right back."

Chopper sprinted toward the house and disappeared inside before she had moved from the spot he'd left her in. She really liked him. He was giving and showed a protective side that might have scared her if she didn't think she knew him a little better than most. Besides, he was a long-time friend and co-work-er of Zed's, which allowed her to lower her guard and enjoy learning and ex-ploring the personality of Chopper, Darrell Frazier. She could feel the energy of something new sizzle along her nerve endings, and wasn't that both exciting and scary.

Several hours later, Felicity snuggled into her bed and thought of how much of a gentleman Darrell was even though he made it abundantly clear he wanted her on every level. He was already possessive and protective. That stupid grin she had tried to control all night after seeing Chopper was free to expand to almost schoolgirl proportions.

It was late, and Felicity was tired, but she'd never sleep if she didn't do a little squealing before trying to close her eyes. That led to more salacious thoughts, and opening the drawer in her nightstand, she grabbed her trusty stress reliever and thought of the gruff, all-man who seemed to have muscles everywhere held together with impish energy she didn't mind admitting reeled her in without resistance.

It was nice to be liked for herself and not for what assets she brought to the table, professionally. Sure, colleagues had said they admired her stamina, her persistence, her skills, and her calm demeanor in a crisis, but no one looked past her "day job." Darrell "Chopper" Frazier did. In fact, he saw her first and her skills drew his attention somewhat later. It gave her a boost that she so desper-ately needed.

They had spoken of their approaching options for the future, but Felicity had already decided that if Chopper stayed here, so would she. Unless her job and its demands became more than he was willing to deal with, she wanted to stay with him, too. Felicity hoped he could handle her stressful job because he was impressive in his own right. He didn't need her income to enhance his lifestyle, and in her experience, so many men were leaches. He didn't attempt to hop in her pants. She'd dated men who thought they were the consummate lover and should be loved at every opportunity. Felicity shook her head.

No, Chopper was confident and viral, but not pushy or assuming his self-declared merit was enough for things like intimacy without building his rela-tionship first. A man who put aside his close friend, his next job and his other options when he left the service so he could search for her? No woman could do less than give him a chance.

A man like that could be a keeper. He wouldn't own straying eyes or need to be in an open relationship, neither situations she could handle. He was the most impressive date. Yes, she was calling tonight a date. She hadn't had one in longer than she could say, and none that made her feel this excited for the next chapter. She had never spent as much time just getting to know someone before they tried to insinuate themselves in her life. Felicity resolved to give them a chance and not self-sabotage. Not that she was prone to do that, but she had been gun shy.

Felicity hoped he was up for the challenge as she gave in to the thoughts of what being with a man like Chopper would be like, how he would want to know all about what excited her, what made her long for his touch, and what that touch would feel like on her skin and other intimate places. Felicity had been with a few men, but she allowed her imagination to run free as the vibrator stimulated her bits, taking her to orbit in orgasmic delight in only a few moments. She drifted into sleep with a smile on her face.

THE FOLLOWING DAY WAS Sunday, and while Felicity never liked to run, she made herself leave her home gym and run one day a week. That day was Sunday, offering her the rest of the day to relax as a reward to herself for sticking to her routine. Working for thirty minutes on her universal invigorated her. Running wore her out. So as she was finishing her run, her first reward was to cool down, walking the dock closest to the house she rented.

Sitting when she had sufficiently cooled down, Felicity watched the active inlet. Birds, float planes, boats of all kinds, and an occasional pod of whales following herring or dolphins went by, bringing with them a sense of peace. There weren't many emergencies in Felicity's practice but dealing with everyone's problems could be difficult. She loved her work, but without someone to decompress with, it could bring on a heaviness she hadn't experienced before.

Almost all her peers were married or engaged both in and out of the military. She had found no prospects until her last day in-country on her last deployment. Story of her life. But now, finding Chopper again gave a spring to her step, even after running. Felicity couldn't help the quick grin that spread over her face when she thought of Chopper. Darrell was a solid name if old-fashioned, but Chopper seemed like the man, rough along the edges but sweet and tasty once you get past the gruffness.

"What a beautiful view."

Chills overtook Felicity, and she shivered. She sucked in the cool air and turned to answer him, shading her eyes from the glare of the sun.

"It is. I love it." She looked up, shielding her eyes from the sun.

"I meant you, but the water is nice, too." His hand slid along her upturned jawline and smiled when goosebumps appeared.

"What brings you out here?" She scooted over to make room on her double-sided planed log.

His sweat and musk wafted over her as he sat, reminding her she might stink a bit as well. Some men's musk was offensive, some intrusive, and some she didn't mind. Thankfully, Chopper fell into the manageable category. She wondered what category hers fell into. Shaking her head, she smiled as he gazed into the channel.

"Same as you, morning PT."

"Ah, but I live near here."

"I live about a klick south, so I'm close. Where are you from here? I'm not sure how far down this is from your street."

Felicity pointed to a group of houses along the shelf of land to their right. "I live in the blue and white house there."

"So close, you could watch the ocean from your deck."

"I do, but I've learned some things about myself since coming here. I like to shower when I get home, and I would miss the exhilaration of being here, now. Once I shower, I seem to change focus and go on about my day. Until then, I can be raw and earthy without the trappings of the rest of the world."

"I feel that way when I'm flying. The world can't crowd in on my airtime. The wonders of nature from above are breathtaking. Once I land, it's all over and business as usual, but until I begin the descent, I'm in my own world."

"Unless you are transporting a chatting woman."

"Sometimes, but there was this one flight with a woman that completely enthralled me, and I didn't miss the soul-healing solitude. She filled me another way."

"Wow, what a nice thing to say. I wonder why I haven't seen you here before?"

Chopper took his gaze from the scene before them. "I usually take a flight early on the weekend, but I'm here most weekday mornings."

"Ah. I only run Sunday. I use my universal the other days, and I take Saturday off."

"Why only Sunday?"

"I hate running. I do it once a week because I need to do something different and because I have the excuse to pamper myself the rest of the day."

"We could run together on Sundays."

"What about your early flight?"

"If you could go an hour later, I'm back by then and can meet up. Here."

Felicity nodded. "I'd like that. It's a date."

"No flaking out on me because you don't like to run."

"No, because then I'd miss my reward."

"I could get into that reward system." He paused for a moment before continuing. "Hey, do you want to go to dinner with me? I'm committed this afternoon to a flight, but maybe Wednesday?"

Felicity shook her head. "I wish I could, but I'm pretty busy during the week and can't always commit. What I can do is offer Friday night. I'm either coming back from the neighboring islands after a week of traveling doc, getting here by 3pm, or ending my office hours at 3pm if I'm in town. That gives me some downtime, and then I'll be ready to go out."

Chopper leaned his forearms on his thighs as he continued to gaze at the world laid out before him. "Works for me. The only thing that might get in the way is if I have a flight then, and if the weather turns on the other end, I'm stuck, or if I'm called in on a search and rescue. Occasionally I'm doing runs for Zed's group, but I'll know in advance." He turned to Felicity. "So Friday at Gregorio's?"

Her eyebrows raised, and she gave him a slight smile. "Fancy. But yes, I like that place. I love everything I've eaten there."

"Great. Unfortunately, I have a flight in an hour, so I need to hit the shower and head out. You aren't going to the islands this week, are you?"

"Nope."

Chopper nodded and seemed to relax. "Until Friday then, stay safe." He stood.

"Always."

He leaned down and held her chin before going in for a kiss. Felicity experienced that same zing that went straight to her core when his lips touched hers whenever he touched her at all. "Mmm, a man could get addicted to you, Felicity Torrez." Chopper stared at Felicity for a moment longer before displaying his big grin, nodded in farewell, and headed off toward home.

Felicity stared after him and let the tingle settle over her as she enjoyed the rush this man gave her. Jumping up with more energy than she usually had after a run, she sprinted to the house and headed for the shower. Usually, the end of winter in Southeast was messy, wet, and depressing, but Felicity had a feeling all that weather wouldn't dull her enjoyment this year. She just had a hunch.

CHOPPER LOCKED UP HIS helicopter and checked the security on the other planes. It wasn't his job, but he had a routine pounded into him from years in the military. The fleet was everyone's responsibility, and he was trying to teach that to the pilots coming in learning the ropes before spring and summer. The man who owned the flight company was nearing retirement and rarely flew anymore, so he was content for Chopper to oversee things when he chose to do so.

He'd thought of the job he'd left in Anchorage and the message he'd received about taking up his position again for the season. He loved that area to fly in and would have really considered the job but now that he found Felicity and in his own backyard, he thought he'd accept the three-quarter pilot position with the outfit he was with, donning his search and rescue hat when needed, and do Zed's runs.

If he and Felicity worked out, it would be a mutual decision to move or stay. If they didn't click, he had options because Chopper knew that if he and Felicity didn't work out, he wouldn't be able to stay in the same town with her. Maybe not even the same state, no matter how big Alaska was, but he intended that to be a non-issue. Chopper wanted to more than charm Felicity. He wanted to captivate her, capture her, and claim her. It was a little caveman-ish, but that was how he felt around her.

Chapter 4

This was the one weekend a month that her office took the emergency calls for the hospital in exchange for the hospital doing it the other three weekends in the month. Because there were three doctors in the Remote Indian Health Clinic and Veterans clinic that ran under the same roof, she only had to be on call once a quarter, four times a year, her colleagues taking it once a quarter. Thanks to both federal organizations' negotiation skills and resources in a brilliant team-up, no practice had it better.

Felicity looked at her reflection in the mirror and sighed. There wasn't anything she could do about the timing, and dwelling on the possible call-out was doing nothing but asking for trouble during her date. Felicity had forgotten all about it when she accepted the invitation, and she would not stand him up, but she could already feel herself panicking and mentally trying to pull away.

It was harder to do this time, and Felicity was pleased she had not been successful so far. She took one last look at herself in navy slacks topped with a navy and white cashmere sweater, tweaked an errant curl back in place and turned to pick up her purse.

Driving into Port Refuge on a clear night relaxed Felicity. She enjoyed the moon's reflection off the dark inlet and the snow catching the glimmer and extending its influence on the surrounding blackness. The stars were brightly distinct but further away, giving the impression one was in a planetarium.

There was a nervous excitement in her belly, and her chest was tight with anticipation. The small town was moderately busy, but it was a Friday night. Parking was a bit of a challenge, as always on the island, but survivable. Tonight was no exception, and she had to park several blocks away. Thankful she was never one to put on fancy shoes when sturdy ones would do, so walking along the boardwalk on the historic street wasn't too tricky, just slippery in places because of the rain.

She arrived at Gregorio's and checked the time. Seven on the dot. As Felicity looked up, she saw someone coming in her direction. The hostess. She was about to speak when a deep and now familiar voice spoke from behind her.

"Table for two, Frazier," it said to the hostess. That same goosebump-inducing voice whispered in Felicity's ear. "I love it when a woman is prompt."

She leaned back and replied into the space between them while the woman found their reservation. "And I love it when a man doesn't sneak up on me."

"I walked up behind you, no sneaking involved. I'm just naturally light on my feet." Felicity chuckled. "And, I like to lead when the option is there."

"Now, how did I know that?" Felicity flashed a smile up at him as he slipped his hand down her back, settling in the space just above her backside and rubbed as he gently guided her behind the waiter who appeared and indicated they follow him.

"Because you have a sassy streak that I love," Chopper added as he steered Felicity to her chair and helped her with her coat. "You look beautiful tonight."

Felicity took her seat and accepted her menu. "Thank you, but I just took a shower and changed clothes. I'm sure I look more tired than beautiful."

"You are one hard woman to please. How had I not realized that?" he asked as he took his own seat and menu.

"Chopper..." she scrunched her face up, "I had intended to call you Chopper, but I think I'm more comfortable with Darrell when we are in a place like this. Is that a problem?"

"Not a problem, but no one has called me that since I was in school. My family calls me DJ or, more often, 'Deej.'"

Felicity crinkled her brow. "Yeah, I don't think that suits you. Darrell works for me if you don't mind."

"Nah, so long as you know I might have to process you're talking to me in the beginning, I'm good with it."

She nodded. "Great. And back to the original statement. I don't think I'm hard to please, but I might be hard to compliment. Say I'm odd, but I've never been one to trust a compliment as being entirely honest."

"I wonder why that is? Regardless, I'll be sure to be totally truthful whenever I pay you a compliment."

"Why do I feel like that is a two-edged sword?"

"Well, because the compliment will sometimes sound like the opposite. Like I might say, your shoes look sturdy. Now, that wouldn't be a criticism because I happen to think women walk in too much risky footwear, but it might sound like it. See?"

"Yes, I can see your point. Just don't say things that aren't true to make me feel better because it has the opposite effect on me."

"Agreed, and you have to agree not to dissect everything I say for a hidden message because there isn't likely one. Unless you are captured. Then expect there to be at least one." His slow grin drew a relaxed laugh from Felicity.

"I'll try to remember that if I'm ever captured."

"Good, but for the record, getting captured is going off-plan." He winked, and her heart melted. "We have covered warfare and being too nice. Can we move on to your week?"

She laughed again and nodded. "Nothing new, just busy. I told you we're in a clinic that houses the remote version of a Veteran's and a remote Native Health clinic and high risk. It was a good blending. Many of our Vets are Native Alaskan, so after insurance, the VA gets billed for some things, the IHS gets billed for others. They pool resources when available, our updates to systems and equipment are timely, we get paid well, and except for a few times a year, we don't do emergency call out."

"How many doctors in your practice?"

"Three." She gave him a frustrated sigh. "Unfortunately, this is my weekend."

"And how often do you get called out on your weekend?"

"That's just it. I can usually get through most of Saturday, but Friday evening and Saturday evening are usually busy, and I get at least one call. But not until late, so that's good and bad. Sundays are a mixed bag, and it's a toss-up whether I get a call or not."

"Well then, we need to get dinner going, and that way, if it happens, you'll have been fed, anyway."

"Thanks for understanding. Like I said, it's only a few times a year," she reiterated as he hailed the waiter.

"Look, Felicity, it's your job. I'd be a hypocrite if I said anything against your job. I've had plenty of times that duty called, and no matter where I was, doing whatever, with whomever, I had to drop and run. If you only did it to me three or four weekends a year? Piece of cake. So long as you don't get upset if I get a rescue call and have to do the same on occasion."

Felicity shrugged and grabbed her wine glass. "We have fifty-two weeks, right?"

That slow, easy grin appeared. "Absolutely."

The meal was ordered and progressed without interruption, much to their relief.

"The dinner was excellent as always. I'm glad I tried the Pastitsio. Not exactly like the lasagna I'm used to, but very close. The spices were different, and I wasn't sure I would like it, but I did." Felicity allowed her plate to be taken by the waiter.

"This Moussaka was equal to the best I've ever had, which, by the way, wasn't in Greece. It was in New York. I was... exploring just outside the city and found a café that made a variety of Greek and Mediterranean dishes. I swear I thought I'd died and gone to heaven."

"Do you have Greek in your background?"

"With a last name of Frazier?" He shook his head. "Not that I know of, but even though my mother says we are Americanized Scots, my heritage comes with a good appetite. Over the years, I have learned to appreciate different cultures and their cuisines."

"I guess you have been to most regions of the world. That is something I want to do, see more of it."

"I'd love to be there when you witness some of the incredible sights of other countries. Where have you been?"

"Mmm, I've been to many places in the U.S., but I've not been to Canada, oddly enough. I plan to remedy that this summer. Nor Mexico, which is odd since I was in Texas, but of course, I've been to Germany, Kuwait, Turkey, and the areas around there. One plane stop in Ireland and one in the UK, but I want to see more. At one time, I was going to do the traveling doctor thing, you know, Doctors Without Borders, but I've had enough of worrying about my safety when I go to bed and all those with me."

Darrell got thoughtful. "I know what you mean. I loved my job and love continuing it with Zed on occasion. Using my skill for search and rescue gets my blood pumping. But after twenty years of putting myself on the line and seeing my teammates at risk, the adrenaline rush was more bitter than sweet."

"Exactly. I loved it until I didn't. Now I'm trying to decide if I want to keep this job or go somewhere else or do something else. It has been a little harrowing in the early days. Hard to get your foot in the door with the distrust some people have."

"Like what?" Chopper put his hand out and laid it on Felicity's wrapped around her wine glass. "No, wait. Let me settle the bill, and we can go for a walk. It's nice outside and not too chilly."

"I'd like that."

He waved down their server, and as he pulled out his wallet, he said, "Thank you."

Felicity smiled. Her expression showed confusion. "For?"

"Not trying to pay for dinner even though you could. Hell, you probably make more than me, but it's nice when I don't get guff for paying the bill."

"Women do that?" She took the last drink of her wine, and set her glass down, reached for her water.

"You wouldn't believe how many. Now, I've taken out women who said nothing, but it's usually because they didn't want to pay, and I respect that. If I ask you out, I pay, and I don't want a stand-off in the restaurant about it. So, thank you for not putting me through that."

It was quiet while the waiter went to retrieve the ticket. "You need to find a better class of date, Mr. Frazier. Women either less intimidated by you or more secure in themselves."

"Why, thank you. I believe I already have."

He winked in her direction, and Felicity could feel the heat rise into her cheeks. Her whole body tingled in response to the sexy gesture. There was just something hot about a man who winked. She excused herself to the bathroom, hoping to cool her face, relieve her bladder, and pull herself together.

She mentally chastised herself. You have to get a grip, girl. This guy seems like he's had his fair share of dates and likely one-night stands, of which you are not. Go slow. Take it easy. You have time to learn about him and to explore this attraction.

Having gained her control back and put things back into focus, Felicity felt better. However, her first glance up as she left the ladies' room was to see Darrell watching for her return. That slow, easy smile when he saw her, the one she had come to associate with Chopper, on full view for all to see. And her resolve to go slow wavered.

Sometimes he was Darrell the interesting, graying at the temples, retired military hottie, and sometimes, like right now with his smile turning distinctly hungry, was Chopper. The hard-working, highly skilled been there done that, helicopter pilot. Both were wickedly tempting in their own right. Both were equally dangerous in their own right, and both were ready to take her for a bit of fun. She used to be an adventuresome girl. She could be again.

As Felicity arrived back at the table, Darrell, never taking his eyes off her, asked, "Ready?"

She nodded. It was the best she could do because this man took her breath away. And that little freshen-up she had been able to do in the bathroom needed repeating. She would need to carry extra underwear if she spent too much time in Darrell's company. And she hoped that little problem continued. It felt good to be attracted to a man who obviously felt some of the same draw to her as she had to him. The night was young. She couldn't wait to see what would happen next.

Chapter 5

Chopper shook his head. This woman was turning him inside out. She didn't hide her true self, unlike most women he'd dated, she was open about her thoughts. It was incredible to feel that trust she put in him to share herself with someone she had only met a few times. True, they had spent hours together in several situations, but he knew what a gift that was. Chopper was an open book. The only thing he wouldn't discuss was the still confidential missions and the ones that had gone sour. Those times when he'd lost teammates, close friends to warfare. Those were things he had to work out on his own. Find where he could store them in his memory banks for safe keeping. Alone.

Felicity was a different kind of person than he typically dated. She could speak on any subject he brought up. Her breadth of knowledge was extensive, and her convictions and beliefs were well thought out. She unconsciously mixed honesty with naivete, and with her show of logic and intelligence, she presented a powerful combination of women.

She wasn't one to spout radical rhetoric. It was clear she had researched and explored her views on controversial subjects. And equally apparent when she didn't have a formed opinion because she wasn't interested in creating one.

Felicity laughed easily and was comfortable in her own skin. She wasn't wrong when she'd called him out on his previous dates. With few exceptions, he did need to find a better class of women to date. He had been as shallow and easy-going as the women he dated. If truth be told, except for some of the distinctly macho thoughts on paying for his date, and his penchant to be somewhat possessive and protective when he was seriously dating, he was like the women he dated. It was a hard pill to swallow.

Time to admit that he attracted the same type of person that he was back then. But now, during this time of his life with Felicity, it was entirely different. She excited him in every way possible. His last serious dating, as in exclusive dating, was almost five years ago. He intended to keep this one as his last relationship.

When Zed lost Chrissy, his first wife, the devastating loss was all he could focus on. He'd loved Chrissy like a sister, the entire team did, and that made it very difficult for them all for a while. Jacqueline, his girlfriend at the time, couldn't understand.

That ended their relationship, and frankly, it had opened his eyes to what he needed in a long-term commitment. He needed compassion, understanding, patience, and he needed his woman to be as possessive and protective of him as he was of her. That had yet to happen, but it might happen with Felicity. What he did know was he couldn't go into a relationship with less.

When Felicity came out of the bathroom, he'd already made a quick trip to the men's room to relieve the pressure built up behind his zipper to remain socially acceptable. She took his breath away. Even though he kept telling himself to go slow, hold down the attraction while he got to know her, his cock didn't listen. He'd been acutely aware of his equipment needing to be rearranged many times throughout dinner.

It wasn't a bad problem to have unless you needed to walk through a restaurant full of people. Fortunately, it was still cold enough outside to need a jacket. He'd worn his nicer coat that was just long enough to cover the obvious bulge found front and center. And if he allowed her to walk out ahead of him, as he would normally until they go to the door, that would work.

Taking her hand, his fingers tingled at the contact. His gut clenched, and he knew it meant something. He wasn't in the field, waiting for his order to do a pickup or drop off. He wasn't transporting important cargo or joining his teammates on the ground to secure their position so they could fly out of there. And yet, that same sensation swamped his senses. She did that to him.

She had just hinted at there being some scary times in her first months working on the surrounding islands. His ears perked up.

"Now tell me how much danger you're typically in while doing your job on the surrounding islands?" Felicity was quiet, but Darrell had no intention of allowing that quietness to equal avoidance of the question. "Felicity?"

He lowered his voice and firmed his delivery. His Doc needed to learn early on that there would be a few non-negotiable areas, and her safety was in the top two categories.

"My heart galloped a few times when a rifle would come out because they didn't know who I was. And once when a wife wanted her children seen after being sick for a while, and when I arrived, the husband refused."

Chopper could hear the tension in his own voice but couldn't relax it. "What happened?"

"Well, in the rifle incident, the man's wife came out and took his gun from him. He said he'd see a male doctor. He wanted to have his male anatomy checked for problems and, to quote him, 'no woman was coming near him but his wife.'" She shrugged. "I got him a male physician, my co-worker."

"And the children?"

"After we talked, it was disclosed he wasn't the children's father, so he couldn't, by law, stop the exam."

"And he just let you do your job?" he asked incredulously.

"I wasn't alone. I was with the VPSO. Village Police and Safety Officers are the best in the bush. They know everyone. I could have called the Troopers, but it takes them longer to get to you."

"Do you carry a gun?"

"There is one in the office we have on the island, and I carry it, unloaded, in the SUV for bears and wolves, mostly, but I don't carry it inside the homes." She looked at Darrell's determined face. "I am cautious. Those two incidents were surprises."

"I know you can fire a weapon, but when was the last time you've gone to the range?"

"Last time, I had to qualify before going on my last deployment, so close to three years. But before you say I need to go, I don't want to use the gun unless absolutely necessary and never on people." Chopper knew his Doc was adamant because she began to walk faster.

He shortened his stride and slowed his step. Since they were holding hands, she had to slow by necessity. "I get it, but I need to know you can hit what you aim at. I'll worry, now that I know, what can happen until I verify for myself that you can hit what you aim at."

"Chopper..."

"Humor me? I promise not to do more than see you have a sure aim. Please?"

Felicity turned to stare at Chopper and his pleading eyes. After a long moment, she nodded. "Okay. Thanks."

"Thank you."

He leaned down and kissed her with relief. He fell into the kiss, knowing he had never felt this way about a woman before. Not even close. Releasing her so they could breathe deeper, he traced her cheek and jawline.

His lips still close to hers, he asked, "Why did you say thanks?"

"What?" Her face scrunched up in confusion then cleared. "Oh, because I appreciate you are worried about me. Not something I normally deal with."

"Well, you have friends here now. I can promise you I will not let up on making sure you are happy, healthy, and safe. Sometimes to the point of frustration. You'll have to suck it up and deal with it, I'm afraid, because that is one thing I won't change."

"They warned me," said Felicity with a laugh.

"Yeah? It must have been Alli, and she's right. I'll try not to smother you but expect me to pay attention."

"And Kayla. She says River drives her crazy sometimes with his obsession with keeping her safe. Especially since the problems they had last year. I didn't hear the whole story but not sure I want to know. She drops little statements, and I'm sure, one of these days, she'll tell me the whole story."

Chopper nodded. This intensity on his part had never happened before, and he'd be damned if he didn't take his time and explore what it was that they had. They clicked. She had taken the words out of his mouth several times, and he had thought the same things she'd said. They complimented each other.

He was a cynic. How could he not be after most every year he'd spent in the military, be it Army, Navy, or Marines, in the field or waiting to be called into action? He had rarely done or wanted to do a typical job. Now he found himself glad he only had stateside missions. Leaving Felicity to spend months in-country somewhere didn't have that same allure now.

He knew instinctively that he would want to be home with her most nights if they were together. And for the first time in his adult life, that sounded good. He smiled and shook his head. Zed would approve.

"What are you smiling about?" Felicity sounded amused.

"Us. Well, I thought that for the first time ever, I might want what Zed has. I'm not sure about the four kids part, but a place to put down roots never appealed to me before."

Felicity spoke into the quiet night. "And it does now?"

Chopper turned to look at her speaking almost reverently. "Yeah, I think I just might consider it."

They walked in predominant silence, pointing out small things of interest but content in just being together. Chopper had grabbed onto Felicity's hand when they left the restaurant, but he'd drawn her in closer to him, and now his arm was around her waist. She leaned into his shoulder the further they walked. When they turned to retrace their steps, her cell went off.

"Eleven o'clock. That is probably the dreaded call-in. The ER must be filling up." She spoke on the phone. "Injuries up at a winter retreat. They expect a handful of injured people."

"Well, we knew it would happen. Let's get you back." Chopper's phone went off. He answered and soon pocketed his phone. "Looks like they need additional transport. Logging is still closed, and the fisheries are in a lull, so no one close by. I took some of them out there yesterday. It looks like they're calling all available birds, which means all two of us right now. Since you're going in, I should help out if I can."

"Sorry that I ruined the evening."

"Nah, I'd have been requested even if you weren't on call. Would it have bothered you if I had gone?"

"Of course not."

"I didn't think so. Let's get back. I need to grab some things from my house and gas up before I take off for the camp."

Felicity's phone rang again, as did Chopper's. When they were done with their conversations, both looked at each other. "The last time I flew with you, we were going out to see what we could do to help. Guess you're taking me up again for the same thing."

"Yep, looks like. Glad you have field training."

She nodded briskly, her professional face sliding back into place. "Absolutely. I have to grab some supplies from the hospital. Can you pick me up from there on your way to the helicopter?"

"Done." He stopped her before she got into her car.

"I need some incentive. If I don't just get one more in, I'll be distracted." He leaned closer and, without slowing his descent, kissed her. It was hungry and yet gentle and much too short.

He placed his forehead on hers. "To be continued. Now get going." With a wave, she drove off, thinking so much for that awkward end of date kiss and goodbye. Sighing because the taste of him was divine if unsatisfying, Felicity refocused. She could drool later. It was time to change her thinking and get to work.

FELICITY FLEW OVER with Chopper, no longer Darrell when he was in the bird. He was all business, and Felicity appreciated that. It allowed her to turn off the overpowering libido that would distract her when she worked. Not a problem she'd dealt with in years. They said very little on the way over to the neighboring island.

"Why did they call you? We have a Medi-flight helicopter."

"In Yakutat. They had a call a couple of hours ago and will probably overnight in Juneau. The weather is closing in up there. We need to get in and get out as soon as because the weather is coming our way."

Chopper looked to the sky as if to validate his statement. Felicity looked too. She could still see stars. "Any idea what we have for numbers?"

He shook his head. "Nope. Just know the four I dropped off yesterday seemed well packed. We talked about it, actually. Two were prior military, and although it was some years ago, they still carried a good ruck."

"But they aren't the only ones?"

"No. There were some already there that had the coffee on when we arrived. I grabbed a cup, then came back."

Felicity chuckled. "Is that your fee for your rescues? Coffee and food?"

"Works for me. From you, however, I'll want something else." His voice had taken on a deeper, darker essence, his meaning clear. Felicity shivered.

"I don't owe you. You're flying for someone else."

But she wanted him to demand that fee for services rendered. It would be a kind of payment for both of them. Damn, there went her control again. Felicity wiggled uncomfortably in her seat. She risked a side glance, and the man was grinning broadly.

"True, but I am taking you over. A courtesy reward is customary."

"And just what would you think is appropriate?" she asked as she repositioned again.

Chopper kept his eyes ahead like he was driving a car. "Something wrong? Sitting on something?"

"I'm fine. How long before we get there?"

Chopper had the good grace not to smile again. He nodded ahead. "See that little light up ahead?"

"Yes."

"That's it."

No more time to talk. They landed, assessed, reported back using the helicopter radio because the cloud cover was thickening, and they were in a forest of trees. Those were two huge deterrents of the satellite phone.

"Drums would be more effective than these things," said Felicity as she tossed the phone back in her pack.

"Works great on top of the mountain," said Chopper as he helped several others move patients around as Felicity triaged.

She noticed he never left her side for more than a few minutes, and she appreciated his watchfulness. She didn't really worry about anything, but a woman alone in a group of men might have garnered some remarks about ability. She'd heard it all before, and the camps were no different from the military. They lacked the belief a woman could do the job when push came to shove. Chopper didn't allow anyone to get in her way, including himself.

"I'll try to remember that for the next time you take me on a rescue and make sure we land on a mountain. This one is bad he needs to go in our transport. Open compound fracture and possible internal injuries."

Within fifteen minutes, she had assessed the four men who had been injured in a rockslide helped by heavy, wet snow in various stages of melting. "These two don't appear to be badly hurt. This one may have bruised kidneys and a couple of fractures. This one with his nasty fracture and likely internal injuries will come with us. Evidently, he was in the front."

She stopped to stretch and supervise the moving of the wounded campers. Chopper chatted with the leader of the group of ten men. "You good until tomorrow when we can send you a boat?"

"The others don't want to go home. The four that you brought yesterday weren't any of the ones in the accident. These were single campers. But we would appreciate you sending someone over to grab their gear in case they need it."

"I'll fly over late morning after we know their status. They need their wallets and documents like passports if you can gather them. Probably cell phones as well."

The flight back was taken up with the two heaviest injured in their helicopter with the other transport behind them carrying the remaining two with the P.A. they brought with them.

"You good back there, Felicity?"

"We're good."

"Alright, I'm going to get us the hell outta Dodge because the weather is moving in. Hang tight."

"Roger that."

Chapter 6

It was 5:00 a.m. before Felicity unlocked the door to her waterfront house. Unlike her usual routine of dropping her things into the armchair by the door and walking onto the deck to inhale the calming ocean breeze, she went straight into the bedroom. Felicity hadn't been this tired since leaving the Army. About three o'clock in the morning, she cursed her missed opportunity yesterday for a nap. She and Darrell had parted company at the landing pad. The ambulances took her and the patients to the hospital, and he got his helicopter and himself home.

Felicity was glad she didn't have to unlace boots, or she'd have fallen into bed with everything still on. Instead, she toed off the tennis shoes she always had in her car, stripped the borrowed scrubs, and crawled out of her panties and bra. Felicity paused, briefly considering a night shirt before she fell into the bed naked, threw a blanket over her exhausted body and fell into a dreamless sleep.

It was Saturday afternoon when Felicity woke to the loud knocking at her door. After two, she rolled over and considered not answering, but that gravelly voice she had reveled in listening to last night called to her through the door.

"Felicity, I know you're in there. I brought food. Open up, sugar."

She was suddenly hungry for food and Darrell's company. "Coming," she called back.

Felicity threw her suddenly too-short robe on and walked to the door, knowing she looked pretty bad. Serves him right for coming uninvited., she grumbled under her breath. And then she grinned. She was glad he did. But she wouldn't tell him. She imagined this was one of the telltale signs that showed he was interested in a woman, his bossiness. As she opened the door, she couldn't suppress the smile that spread across her face.

"I didn't have any flights today because the weather is too bad, so I thought you'd appreciate some breakfast."

"What about the people in the camp?"

"Sent a boat. You going to let me in, sugar?" Felicity stared at him for a few seconds and then waved him in, closing the door behind him.

"Make yourself at home. I'll be right back."

"I don't mind that you just got up. When did you get in?"

"Can you believe, not until five? I might have slept the day away if you hadn't come by. No, I need to dress. Maybe run a comb through my hair and grab a toothbrush."

Darrell chuckled. "Not on my account."

She rolled her eyes. "I'll be right back."

Felicity tried hard to stroll back to her room with minimal success if the male chuckle that followed her was any indication. Once the door closed behind her, she charged through her closet for casual, decent clothes. She had them, but for some reason, she couldn't find them. And what happened to the person she was last Saturday morning? She would never have had a light, quippy conversation with a man who stood in her front room when she looked a mess. She wouldn't have opened the door or let him in, for that matter. Then again, it wouldn't have been Chopper.

Comfortable wasn't the word because Darrell Frazier flustered her. Not by anything he did, really, but just by being who he was, affecting her the way he did. Rushing through what she felt were the minimum requirements, she walked back out to be met by the most delicious grilled halibut sandwich, seafood chowder and fries.

"Since you're on call this weekend, and I'm weather grounded, I thought you'd like something brought in."

"This is heavenly. You got this from the Seafood Shack? Aren't they closed by now?" She reached for a fry.

His ever-ready smile appeared. She saw the hint of a dimple, and that made Felicity smile. "Yep, but the waitress likes me there. I ran into River Bennett and Kayla. They said you'd met."

"Yes, actually, we have. We met through Alli." She took a bite of her sandwich and moaned.

"He said they had come to see you a few times because they were trying to have a baby."

She finished chewing. "Is that what they said?"

"Yep. River said Kayla is hopeful because she's missed two cycles." He bit into his sandwich. "I told them there was an OB in town because I've transported for deliveries before. Glad I don't do that often. I didn't want them to think they had to go to Seattle for a doctor."

"Hush, you dreadful man. Delivering babies is my reward after going one week a month to the island and no vacation in two years. I'm delivering Alli's baby."

He nodded. "So I hear. Sorry, I'll send them to you, then."

"Only friends. I'm a family doctor and not an obstetrician, but the occasional baby makes me happy."

"Just don't deliver your own. I'm not sure I could handle that kind of efficiency." Chopper shuddered and then seemed to realize what he said. "No vacation in two years? What's up with that?"

Felicity swallowed her bite. "Nowhere I wanted to go."

"Maybe go see your family?"

Felicity leaned back in the dining chair. "They're in Portland. Before the last doctor left, I took a four-day weekend and added one more day to visit them. But they're busy too. My brothers are gone doing their own thing, and my parents are busy with their lives."

Wadding the food wrappers and shoving them in the paper bag, Darrell stood to take the trash and realized he didn't know where it was. He held the bag up, and she responded. "Under the sink."

"If I had known you were here," he said, "I'd have made a beeline every break I had."

"We didn't really know each other. We still don't."

Darrell grabbed her hand and lead her into the living room. He sat on the sofa, bringing her down to sit beside him. "We have a connection. Had one after the first time we met. I felt it. Didn't you?"

"I did but didn't think I should or could act on it. I was getting out, going in another direction. For all I knew, you were going to stay in the Marines or some service for many more years."

"We missed some time, and maybe we needed to know there was something between us we shouldn't ignore. I just know that I've dated all kinds of women, but nothing worked. I didn't really try to make them more than dates.

Once I met you, you were always there in the back of my mind. So much so that I haven't dated another woman since I left you that night in Kuwait."

"Darrell, things are different for me now." She slipped her hand out from under his, placing them in her lap. "I have different goals than when I was on active duty."

"So are mine. Let's explore those things together." His hand landed on her thigh, closing over her hand, entwining his fingers with hers. "Tell me what you want out of life."

"That's just it. I don't know entirely. I like living here, but I don't know if I want to stay working for the Feds or for anyone."

"Okay, so we explore hanging your own shingle. I like it here."

"But what if I want to leave?"

"Do you?"

Felicity shrugged. "I like it here, but honestly, it's harder to work here than lots of other places. And there is little access to so many things. It's almost too sheltered here."

"Harder in your present situation or harder alone?"

Felicity appreciated that Darrell was trying to accommodate her indecision. "That's just it. I don't really know. Getting out there on my own and finding that I can't do it would be financially devastating, and my pride would take a big hit."

He leaned back, looking thoughtful. "I understand the hesitancy. It's a big step. For me, I don't mind working under someone else's umbrella. I don't really want the headaches that regulations and those fine details would bring. I can cut and run if I want, too. It might be different if I knew I was staying. In fact, if I were staying, it would be because I had someone to share my life with, have a family with. Then, I would do my own thing, run my own hanger."

"That doesn't sound very reliable."

He gave her a comical look of incredulity. "Don't forget, I retired from the military after twenty-one years. I've been ultra-dependable. All I'm saying is if you want to try something new, I'm there. I don't want to lose you before we have explored this thing." He eased her hair further from the front of her face and tucked it behind her ear. "I want to spend some time with you. You have me all wrapped up in knots."

Felicity nodded and leaned into his palm that rested on the side of her face. "Me too."

"Yeah?"

She nodded slightly. "Yeah."

He leaned down, and this time gave her a second to pull back before completing contact. It started easy but soon morphed into much more than a casual touching of lips. Felicity leaned into the kiss, trying to pull more of Darrell into herself. He took more from her as she offered it. He was kissing the neck she eagerly exposed for him. She heard his breath catch when she ran her hands under his tee-shirt.

"You want me to stop, sugar?" he asked, his gentle tones laced with tight control.

"No." She lowered her head when she kissed his neck, and as he angled it giving her even more access, she moaned at the delicious chills galloped over her skin.

"Please, don't stop," she said as her nipples grew stiffer in his hands. Felicity gave herself over to the feeling of desire. Something she hadn't experienced to this degree in a long time, if ever.

DARRELL DIDN'T EVER think he would feel this way about a woman. He wanted it, thought about it, even tried to make it happen but what he was experiencing with Felicity was something totally new. Even long-term girlfriends never reached this deep in his soul. This woman would be easy to fall in love with. Hell, he was half in love now. What really scared the hell out of him was that these feelings didn't scare the fuck out of him.

Her smooth, soft skin was warm, her face was flushed hot, and he wanted more than to touch her. He wanted to see what he was touching. See her exquisite body. She was fit, he could tell, but not in a hard, angular way like his body was. His hands moved up and under her shirt, accompanied by Felicity's moan and her attempt to get closer.

"We need to move this out of the living room, sweetheart. You have a big front window."

Suddenly, she came to herself enough to break away and stand, "I'm not going to wait for you to get some kind of conscience and change your mind."

Bold as you please, she grabbed his hand and led him to the bedroom. The bed was mussed, and it was kinda sexy to crawl in the bed she just crawled out of not long ago. There were clothes scattered everywhere, and for once, all of his freakishly stringent neatness faded to the background. He couldn't have cared less. She dropped his hand.

Darrell followed her to bed, stripping as he went, adding to the disarray on the carpet, feeling only a twinge at the sacrilege. Felicity had the same idea and was down to lingerie by the time she was to the bed. Off went the panties, and the bra followed quickly behind, all before he could say he liked to undress his women.

He leaned into her standing in her full glory and told her in a possessively stern voice, "I like to undress my women, sweetheart."

Was she dipping her chin in embarrassment? Submission? Acceptance?

Then her chin went back up. "Next time."

Then she smiled a sassy, slight uptick of her lips. He wanted to smack her ass for displaying her sass, but he also didn't want to discourage it. It was adorable, and it told him she was at ease and ready to take their relationship up a notch.

As he stared at her body, all thoughts of protest died in his throat. She was lightly tanned, obviously manufactured because of the lack of readily available hot sun here. She had smooth, unblemished skin, and her women's attributes left him tongue-tied.

Well-honed muscles were seen when she moved her arms and legs, flexing them. Her belly was soft, and a petite pooch showed itself, sexy as hell, like her, and he knew he could tease her later about it, and she wouldn't mind. Powerful thighs were long and lean, leading up to the most enticing trimmed muff he had ever seen. There was a landing strip for his cock when he flew in between those slightly puffy lower lips.

"You are so perfect. I'm afraid I'm going to destroy that perfection." He whispered in an almost worshipful way.

"You have more muscles than I've ever seen in my bed before," she whispered back, "but I'm tougher than you think." She leaned back and lay on the bed.

He laughed at that. "Let's see what other record we can break today. How many orgasms have you had during one session?"

"Two, mostly because that's all I could get before they were on to the next attraction. You looking to break that record? I'm willing for you to try, flyboy."

Chopper grunted. "Boy, huh? Let me see about that." He nodded. "Scoot back on the bed. I've had enough of only looking. I need to touch."

She rolled over and crawled to the center and leaned back on her forearms. He slid onto the bed behind her and loomed over her half-supine body. Felicity reached for his cock, stand at attention, ready to be put into action. He moved her hand out of the way. "Lay all the way down, sugar. I'll let you have a turn, but I like to lead the way to start."

As she slowly laid down again, his fingers roamed up her inner thigh, light feathery touches to excite her. He leaned down over her and gently kissed her eyes, moving on to her cheeks and her nose, a brief stop at her lips and then her chin, her throat, that little place behind her ear. Chopper kissed and licked every bit of skin he could before return to take her lips. The kiss was consuming, tongues quickly intertwined, battling for supremacy and retreating only to surge into a new entanglement.

His cock was so damn hard it hurt, and he had so much more to do. By the cute squeaks and moans his woman was making and the dry humping she was trying to do to his leg, she was as aroused as he was. He lowered to give her breasts a touch of magic, and she arched toward him and his mouth. He tugged in ever-increasing sharpness, and she simply moaned louder.

"You like a little ache, sweetheart? I can do that for you. How much, hmm?"

Her cry of neediness was his answer, and with an up tilt of his lips, he worked on her nips and plump breasts again, increasing the bite until he felt she was at her limit. He backed off. Moving down her belly to give her poor nips a rest, he came to the concaved areas on her thighs situated on either side of her manicured muff.

Kissing and licking gently, he put two fingers at the top of her landing strip and followed it into the channel where her liquid response was overflowing its banks. Chopper watched Felicity as she bucked the moment he circled her clit and moved on. Seems his girl was very excited. Good. Moving down her lower body, he spread her lips wide and delved into her pink wetness.

His tongue knew just what it was doing, and as he listened to her little whimpers and her moving became more desperate, he decided it was time for the first of many sparkling events. Flattening his tongue, he moved from her little brown back entrance and swept up her channel to her clit where he worried it without stopping.

"Oh, oh, stop, no, don't stop. It's so good. So... ah..." she did not say another word. He slapped her pussy and nipped her inner thigh. Her body went still and then stiffened as she bowed her back and rode the explosion of feelings. He returned to tease her clit until she relaxed.

"Good?"

"So, good,"

Felicity said before Chopper changed his angle, and she immediately fired off again. He did it twice more. This woman was incredibly responsive. He would see how many she could actually do another time. Now was for connecting with his woman on a visceral level.

"Do I need a raincoat?"

"Nope, on birth control."

"Okay, then, but if you're worried about..."

"I'm not. Would you quit talking and start pumping already?"

"Yes, ma'am."

He took it slow. Felicity was tighter than most, but she seemed undisturbed by his girth, so he sunk his member deep. After a few seconds of waiting, he began the long, even strokes, bumping pelvises as he penetrated, picking up speed and some roughness. When he was nearing his orgasm, he leaned up on one side, freeing his hand to tease and taunt her nips.

As he approached his precipice, he slapped her ass twice, enough to introduce the sting and warmth that he knew would start her domino effect and allow him to find his own release. He would introduce ass play another time. When Felicity stiffened again, he let go and grabbed her hips, pounding hard to find his culmination while she was still in the throes of her ecstasy. He grunted as he came. The release was incredible. Exhausting. So damn good. She was perfect.

Recovered and laying on the bed in each other's arms, her arm and leg thrown over his, her head on his shoulder, Felicity sighed. "Have time for a nap?"

"I have until early tomorrow morning, sweetheart."

"Good. We can fill the hours between napping and eating with more sexy time. But I get to start off next time. And I'm not ma'am anymore."

"You're not? Well, we'll see. Close your eyes." And he followed her into sleep.

Chapter 7

During the next few weeks, Chopper and Felicity eased into a routine they could handle. While he wanted to spend every evening with Felicity, it wasn't possible for either of them. Their jobs were sometimes all they could handle and could only deal with peanut butter sandwiches and de-stressing in the evening.

"Are you sure you understand?" Felicity asked Chopper one Friday night when she had to pass on a mid-week dinner invite due to work obligations the coming week.

"I'm sure. We're just learning each other, and whether we want it to or not, it is still on the visitor level in some ways. Both of us try to put on our best face when we can with the other. The thing is, until we can just walk in and make a sandwich and the host isn't trying to find something more classy to feed the other, it needs to be this way."

"I hate when you make sense, and all I want to do is make things work so I can get my way." Felicity crossed her arms in mock irritation.

"And what would 'getting your way' look like?" he asked as he took his shoes off.

"All this early dating weirdness would be over, you know? I want to wake up one morning and know all the important stuff about you, be familiar with your friends, and be unconcerned that my mouth might stumble across a do not disturb area of your life. I just want to skip all the beginning and jump to the middle." She straightened the throw on the sofa.

"Yeah?" He dropped a kiss on her pouty lips. "I agree, sometimes, but I like the exploration, too. And for the record, I love when you get all sassy and want your way even though you know you can't have it."

"I could have most things if I wanted." She turned in a flamboyant twirl, heading for the kitchen to finish the salad. "Sometimes, it's just easier not to push."

He followed behind her. "Yep, I bet you could but not this. This takes time, and you have to allow it to happen." He bent to give her one last peck, "And it will. It is. We're spending most of our free time together, and I think you're more comfortable with me. I feel I know you pretty well already. I know parts of you better than others, I'll admit." He wiggled his eyebrows.

She blushed but continued. "Oh, I don't think anyone knows me too well. I get my way because usually, what I want has been thought out beforehand. So, if I want to have or do something, I just carry on."

"Unless it's something that would put you in danger. You can bet I'll say no to that regardless of how much you have thought it out."

"Well, you could try to stop me."

"I could and will if necessary. You're going to get too sassy one of these days, and I'm going to have to spank it out of you."

"I wouldn't try it. Listen, I know all about your friends, and I am not that kind of girl. There will be none of that in my world." Her half-hearted admonition was followed by a shake of her chopping knife.

"We'll see," answered Chopper as he shoved a cucumber slice into his mouth.

"Yes, you certainly will. And don't think I forgot that you like to introduce a few swats when we have sex," Felicity answered as sharply as the knife she held, chopping harder and smacking his hand as he went in for another slice.

"And you love it. Wait till I add a little anal action." She stalled in her chopping but didn't answer him. He smiled and patted her backside playfully before checking the entrée in the oven.

As was also becoming their habit, Friday nights were dinner, in or out, home for a movie, then sexy time. "I can hold my libido for a while, but then I need to have an outlet, and I don't mean me, a shower and an imagination." Darrell reached for Felicity. She sighed.

"I know. I'm beginning to miss you more than I expected during the days I don't have you with me. It's nice to hear from you in the evenings. Those little "how are you" texts during the day are nice too. A lot of times, I think I wouldn't mind if you dropped by after work, but then I have a tough day, and all I want to do is open a can of soup, shower and go to bed."

"I know, baby. It's hard for me too. I'm a typical guy and usually just scratch the itch and go on. It'll happen. Just be patient."

"I hate when someone tells me to be patient," she sighed in his arms.

A few more weeks passed, and Felicity was done with waiting. It had turned into a trying week, and Darrell had texted her whenever he'd gotten a break. Sometimes it was more than a few times a day, as well as calling her each night to make sure she was home safely and to chat about their day as she ate dinner or got ready for bed. If she was in bed by the time they hung up, she reached into her trusty nightstand top drawer, and after a few minutes with her old reliable friend, she fell asleep.

Tonight was different. When Darrell called to check if she got home safely, she said, "I need you to come and sleep with me."

"Baby, tomorrow is Friday, and I'll be there for the weekend."

"No, I've had a hard week, and I need you to come and sleep with me tonight. Just sleep."

After a few seconds of hesitation, he agreed and was knocking on her door in ten minutes. "That was fast," said Felicity.

"Hey, when my woman calls and asks for me to sleep with her, I don't waste time." Darrell walked inside and turned to secure the door. "Are your windows locked and the back door secured?"

"Yes. I left them locked this morning."

He nodded. "So you haven't checked. You get ready for bed, and I'll lock things up."

"I thought we'd watch a movie or something."

"We can start that, but if you are ready to sleep, when you fall asleep in front of the television, I can just get you to bed."

She laughed. It was a bright, airy sound that went right to his core and warmed his heart. Chopper knew he was falling in love but intended on doing nothing to stop it. He needed to talk to Zed about this whole thing, but tonight, he would do what Felicity needed. He thought it wasn't likely that would ever change. If she called and needed him, he would do all he could to meet that request.

"Okay, you win this time but don't get too excited. I expect to give in only rarely."

"Whatever you say, dear," he responded as he left the front room to check the other windows. Felicity slapped his arm playfully as she passed him on the way to the bedroom. Grabbing her by the waist as she walked in front of him, Darrell kissed her hard. "I could get used to this," he murmured in her hair.

Felicity sobered. "I know. I feel it too."

Dropping another kiss on her lips, he let her go. Sleep. Remember, man, just sleep.

After settling on the couch, he stretched out, pulling his exhausted woman between his legs and rubbed her arms and then laid them across her front in a criss-cross fashion. Felicity sighed and was soon asleep. Darrell watched the movie to the end before maneuvering his body from under hers and scooped her up, placing her in bed.

He hit the bathroom and then stripped before sliding in behind her. She scootched her backside against his jewels, causing Chopper to inhale sharply. After a bit, he had relaxed his cock enough to fall asleep. This was where he wanted to be every night. One day, soon, he hoped.

The following week was Felicity's monthly trip to the surrounding Islands to do her home visit clinics. Chopper looked up at the sky and consulted his weather forecaster. "I'm not sure you should go this morning. Can you wait until the afternoon? I'd be much more at ease with the weather stability."

Felicity put the final items in her bag, and once done, she zipped it up, sat it on the floor and looked at her man full in the face.

"If it's too bad, the pilot will cancel the flight. I've trusted their judgment for nearly two years now. It's okay."

She picked up her bag. Chopper took it from her hands. When she opened her mouth to protest, that left eyebrow of his lifted, his sign that things would not go the way she was headed, such as carrying her own bags. She released it. He kissed her, but it was apparent he was distracted. He set the bag down on the end table. He was particular about things like carrying her bags even though he knew she had to haul her own equipment to many places when he wasn't there.

"Who are you using to get over there today?"

"Inlet Air. Why?" She stepped into his open arms and snuggled in as he folded her tight to his chest. "I told you, I've flown them plenty of times."

"It's just that some pilots tend to take more risks." He kissed the top of her head then laid his cheek there.

"Some pilots are like you, you mean."

"But never with paying passengers. With the military, if we are on the job and it has to happen now, or with my personal safety to get something taken care of, maybe, but never with you."

"Are you saying they take unnecessary chances?"

"Nope. Not saying that at all. Tell you what. I'll fly you over and come back to help Zed. When will you be ready?" He set her away from him as he gathered things for his travel bag he always took with him when flying any distance.

"I'm ready now, but I have reservations with Inlet Air."

"And now you don't. Call Inlet and tell them the truth. Your boyfriend is flying over, so you'll just fly with him."

"Boyfriend, huh? Are we to the public announcements yet?"

"We aren't hiding, are we?" asked Chopper, turning to give her a raised eyebrow again.

"No, but I hadn't really announced it. I mean, people see us, but I have said nothing to anyone.

"I have. Zed and Alli know. River and Kayla know, hell, the whole Zed training team knows, even that little idiot he has for a clerk knows. Ryder Mason, an old friend of ours, knows. A few of the search and rescue team and even the servers at Cache Café knows. Do your co-workers know?"

"They know I have a boyfriend. Just not who you are."

"I'll have to fix that while you're gone."

"No, Darrell, they'll find out in time. Naturally. Organically. Promise me you won't go to the office and identify yourself as my boyfriend."

Chopper smiled. "I won't do that. But Felicity, no matter why you haven't told them, it will come out soon."

She sighed. "Fine, I'll call Inlet and cancel."

"Good. I'll call Zed and give him the low down. He needs a pickup from the off-site training camp this afternoon but not this morning. I have plenty of time to get over there and back before this weather hits if we go now."

"Why can you do it with no problem, but Inlet Air can't?"

"Did I say they couldn't?"

"Oh, I can never win with you. But yes, you all but said exactly that."

Felicity nudged him as she walked behind his sexy body, grabbing his taut butt as she passed. The answering slap to her posterior made her jump and laugh.

Chopper had so many of his daily things in her cottage that he quickly loaded up his bag and grabbed hers from the bedside table. When he met Felicity at the front door, he stopped her from walking out.

"I just don't want anything to happen to you. I'm a better pilot than most because I've had many more hours of experience. And because you are quickly becoming very special to me. I don't know if I would recover if I lost you." The kiss that followed his statement was warm, comfortable, and noticeably possessive. "Besides, it's in my nature to protect what is mine."

AS FELICITY SAT IN the cockpit watching Chopper do his many checks inside and out before leaving, she thought of this morning's conversation. The implication was clear. He considered Felicity his to watch over. Not in a babysitting way but in a caring, manly way. A relationship, lover way and in her experience that usually meant the time was ticking, and the end was near.

She didn't seem to do well once the "dating" moniker was attached, supplanting "going out and having fun." It wasn't the men that began the pull away from commitment. It was her. She didn't realize it at first, but soon, once they were considered an "item," she was backpedaling slowly, but the momentum picked up as the guy began to advance.

She chose intelligent men, so it didn't take too long before they noticed her cooling and when she couldn't identify why they soon found more receptive pastures. Felicity swore to herself that now she wanted to settle down, that if she felt that cold sweat again when she began to fall for a guy, that she would talk about it. She told herself this was that time.

Now, when she needed to put that decision into play, the words were stuck in her throat. She liked Chopper, dammit, a lot. The thought that she would push him away only made her more worried and hesitant. She was going to be gone until Friday afternoon. That would give her enough time to plot her course, pick her words, and build up the courage to have the necessary conversation. She was determined she wouldn't push this one away.

Chopper handed Felicity a set of headphones and nodded that she put it on. Once they were settled comfortably, he said, "Buckle, sweetheart, and you're thinking way too hard over there. I didn't mean to shake you up. The weather is fine. It might get a little wet, and the wind might blow us some, but nothing to be worrying about."

Felicity shook her head at Chopper's concern. She smiled because they were in the helicopter once again, and she automatically thought of him by his nickname. It was growing on her, but a grown man needed to hear his legal name occasionally.

"I'm not worried that you can't get us there. I'm worried that you might get caught in bad weather as you go back home." It was much more than that on her mind, but he'd offered her a perfect segue into a different subject.

"That's why I have my go-bag with me. I have a radio and a satellite phone. A supply of MREs and an OPS bag I keep filled. Plus, the little pack I brought today puts me ready to go camping or trek out if I have to. Remember, I was special ops. I got this and you. Don't ever think I'm not prepared to spend a week or more waiting for help."

Felicity nodded. "Once a soldier, always a soldier. I have MREs too, and a few survival bits in my bag. I never need them, but just in case."

"I know. I checked." He shot her a grin and shrugged his shoulders. Felicity laughed.

The conversation stopped as each fell into their own thoughts. About fifteen minutes into the flight, Chopper spoke again. "That wasn't what you were worried about."

"What?" Felicity looked at him and then shifted her gaze away and shook her head. "No, just thinking about the week ahead."

"I'd believe that if you hadn't hidden your face from me so quickly. We have time. Talk to me."

"It's nothing." From her peripheral vision, she saw his mouth tighten.

"And that is not the truth. Felicity, I can put up with many things, but when I can tell you are dishonest with me, it does a number of things. It shows you don't trust me as you should. It highlights that we don't have as good a relationship as I am shooting for. And it says you don't respect me or my opinion."

Felicity groaned. "I didn't want to talk about this now. My plan was to work my courage up, practice my presentation, have things settled in my mind."

"I live by the creed that it's better to face things head-on, deal with it quickly and move on. It's always better to collaborate when there is an option."

She sighed loudly. "Fine. But don't say I didn't warn you."

"We can work it out."

"Maybe." Felicity took a few more moments before she started. "Okay, here goes. You know how I haven't shared about us dating exclusively to others?"

"Yep."

"Well, it isn't that I don't want to date you because I do. It's just that, once it's official, that marks the time I begin to feel closed in. Worried that I don't want to be exclusive. I start seeing the little quirks as irritations instead of the things that attracted me in the first place. I begin to self-sabotage." She looked at her hands and shrugged. "I don't know. Talking about it is hard because I don't really know why." She looked out the side window.

"You run scared."

Felicity shook her head. "I'm not—" Darrell looked at her with a hint of chastisement. She nodded. "Yes."

"Let me ask you a few things. Do you enjoy us right now?"

"So much. I'm afraid I'm going to mess this up, and I won't know how to fix it." She wiped a tear roughly from her cheek. "I want to get past the place where I create problems and pull away."

"Hey, I like you a lot. I guess you could tell that by my scouring the country for you and then the state. I enjoy spending time with you. Now that I know you sort of sabotage relationships once it's official because you are afraid of losing your autonomy, I can counter that. I won't scare easily, and I won't let you, either."

He observed the landscape features for a few moments, then continued. "I didn't want to bring this up yet, but I think now is the perfect time. What I want out of a relationship I haven't ever found for long. I didn't run from commitment, exactly. I usually found that our goals weren't the same. It's hard in the military to find a mate who will stick it out with you when you deploy for indeterminate time frames to undisclosed locations, followed by an inability to discuss it once you are home. Damn hard."

Chopper was quiet as he maneuvered through a dense bit of terrain while trying to stay out of the weather that was closing in on them. He glanced quickly in her direction, and he gave her a reassuring smile.

"I am more attracted to you than I have ever been with another woman. You're the complete package, and I want you. You're confident and secure in your world yet, cede to me when we're doing things together. You don't mind that I like to take the lead in the bedroom, and I don't mind giving it to you on occasion when you need it."

"That's really a thing with you? It was just natural to let you be the instigator, but I never expected that you'd want it that way all the time."

He nodded. "I do. And I like to be the leader in the relationship, but I find I don't balk when you take the lead on occasion, which is a first for me. I'm an egocentric man, and while it isn't the most attractive trait, it's an honest trait. I like to know what I'm doing in all areas of my life, and I work and study to keep that skill set active. With you, it's natural to want to know all about you, what is important to you. The whole thing. I want to please you."

"You want to please everyone."

"There, you would be wrong. I like to help my friends, I like to do a good job for my own reputation, I like to do pick up flights, search and rescue, come in and save the day, but I don't want to please anyone but you."

"I'm worried I'm going to push you away."

"To avoid that, you will have to communicate more. So will I. I'm used to very short, no strings, dating. With you, I think I want those strings."

"I think I want them too."

Chopper nodded ahead. "We are about to land. Think about what you want and what we've said here. And think about this. I want us to move in together."

She shook her head as though rejecting the thought. "But we've only been seeing each other for less than two months."

"And I miss you when we aren't together," he said without taking his eyes off his control panel and the landing.

"We're together at least Friday, Saturday and Sunday nights, already."

"I want more, Felicity. Let's push your expectations that things will go sour and prove you're wrong."

She leaned her head back against the seat. "My days are so busy. I'm beat when I get home."

"Mine can be too, but sleeping next to you gives me a peace I haven't had in a long time. Maybe not ever. I feel settled. Content. Don't get me wrong, the sex is out of this world satisfying, but being content is a big deal in my life now."

"I feel it too. I wonder if we can do it and survive." Would she be able to grow in her feelings for Darrell instead of closing those sentiments down out of fear of the future?

"We're landing. I want you to promise to think about it, and even if you decide it's too soon, we are still dating, seriously, exclusively. There is no going back on that status unless we both agree. Yeah?"

Felicity watched as Chopper put them down with ease and efficiency, then followed his movements as he shut things down. She unbuckled, and his hand landed on her forearm. "Promise me."

"How can I? I already know how this always goes with me."

He grew severe, and his tone matched. He left her with no doubts he was taking nothing less than her acceptance and agreement. "No, you will not create a self-fulfilling prophecy. We deserve better. Promise me, or I will promise to teach you all about the John Wayne method of getting compliance."

Her eyes grew large, and then she laughed. "That's barbaric."

"No, I can assure you it is effective and fun." He winked. "And sexy as hell."

Her belly flipped in strange anticipation. "Ugh. Fine. How do you always win? Okay, I promise. You can be a bully sometimes, you know that?"

He gave her a mock surprised look and then grinned. "That's bossy. A bully is a whole other creature. Unless you're saying that you're weak, of lesser intelligence, unable to stand up for yourself?"

"Right, that won't ever happen."

He nodded briskly. "I thought not. Okay, hold on while I get down, then climb over here, and I'll help you out on my side. The other side has a muddy area right outside the door."

Glancing out the window, she couldn't see what he was talking about. Felicity shrugged. "Looks okay to me."

"Felicity Torrez, do not do it. I mean it. You might not see it, but I promise it's there.

"Oh, it's fine." She started to open the door.

"Tell you what, if you open that door and find I'm wrong, I'll cook dinner for a week. But if I'm right, you get three swats from me." Thinking fast, she sighed heavily.

"This could get old really fast."

"Thank you, baby."

Once he had gotten down, Chopper took her bag from her and set it on the ground. Reaching his hand up to help her climb out, he pulled Felicity close and gave her a long, hungry, but reassuring kiss. "Mmm, that's what I'm talking about. You don't want to throw that away, woman. It was damn hot."

She was melting where she stood. "No, I don't want to give that up. Okay, I promise to try but don't say I didn't warn you."

"Deal." He nodded toward a clinic vehicle. "Take a quick look on the other side of the chopper and see if you made a good choice or not." He tilted his head in the direction of the other side of the helicopter. Instead, she squatted down and looked under the bird. There it was, a big puddle. He'd landed over most of it, but enough was still exposed on her side that she would not have been able to climb down at the door without getting muddy.

"Okay, Mr. Smarty pants, you were right."

He laughed. "I knew that." He looked ahead in the parking lot. "Looks like your ride is here, and I believe your office on this side of the passage knows you have a hot guy at your beck and call. Before I let you go, I should check your tonsils."

Felicity laughed. "Hey, I'm the doctor."

"Yes, you are, so you check my tonsils. One last time." This time the kiss was goodbye, and when they separated, Felicity picked up her bag from the ground. Chopper popped her on the ass playfully as she walked away.

Her head shot up, and she turned around. "Hey."

He held up his hands in mock defense. "I'm just staying in practice. Never know when I might need to set my woman straight in her thinking."

He laughed as she grumbled and walked away. She was going to miss him. For the first time since she started this job, she wished she didn't have to spend the next four days here. It would go fast, she told herself, praying she was right. Friday couldn't come fast enough.

Chapter 8

It was Friday, and Chopper was glad the week that seemed to last an eternity was over. Three days this week, he'd piloted two long flights a day because the tourism was picking up. He needed to decide soon if he would do one more season as an employee or gather himself and go private. It was a hassle to handle the business himself, but the income would be more than he could ever make now. The real question was, did he want to make that kind of commitment? He'd talk to Felicity about it.

Just that unbidden thinking was so new to Chopper that he had to wonder how she had slid under his skin and taken up residence faster than a parasite. Not a typical comparison, he smiled to himself, and she would have not thought it complimentary, but it definitely illustrated the indisputable fact of his life these days. Without any work on his part, ever since he met the confident doctor, she had him hooked.

She was serious and dedicated, and Chopper understood that. He'd spent the majority of his life dealing with severe issues and situations. She needed to help others. He got that too. He'd felt that calling in the service and continued to answer it with the search and rescue group outside the military.

Felicity was vulnerable, and damn if that wasn't unfamiliar to him. Uncertain about the outcome and yet excited about what lay ahead was a shared trait, and the new yearning for permanency was something they both wanted. Needed. With Felicity, life was more than a means to an end. It was a work of architectural design. He could see the desired goal, the picture of his life in the future, and it now only included Felicity and their plans together.

Chopper checked the clock and walked into his house. He hated that his woman was taking a commercial flight home when he'd told her he could pick her up, but he'd spent the morning looking for a couple of lost teens on Elkhorn Mountain. They'd found them, thank goodness, but it was too late to hop over to grab his lady. She didn't seem to mind when he called to tell her. Felicity had already booked her flight and was home just thirty minutes after him. But he still hated it. He took a five-minute shower before driving into Port Refuge to meet the floatplane.

As he sat on the dock, waiting for her to land, he thought about the test he'd signed up for next month to get licensed for the little buggers. In the military, floatplanes were not used in his area of work. He could fly and was certified to fly just about any craft used in their missions, but now, in the civilian world, there were additional types.

He could fly the two-seaters, helicopters, planes of most sizes, but he was not a jet pilot, nor had he ever had any desire to be. He'd co-piloted a C-130 but only once, and it solidified his desire to stay away from the full-sized planes. He wanted to fly puddle jumpers. They were noisy, smelly but could get in places that his other transports couldn't—on the water. He watched the plane land smoothly then propel to the dock easily. Chopper walked over and tied her off while the pilot got the nose secured.

The two pilots shook hands. "We hit some rough spots coming back. Think your Doc is a little green."

Chopper smiled. "Thanks. Walking on land will fix that."

The door was opened, and the pilot grabbed the bags from his hold while Chopper reached up to hand out the passengers. A young kid who refused the assistance came out first. Then came his Felicity, a little green around the gills. Once she was on deck, a final passenger, a man of questionable means, climbed out, accepting Chopper's arm to help him down.

The odor was noticeable, and the grunge was something he'd experienced himself before. It was the look and smell of a man who had been in the backwoods of nowhere for way too long without a break. His buddies often looked and smelled the same when they came in from some mission that had gone on too long.

The instant understanding of how this man lived life blended with the telltale stench, and Chopper knew why Felicity was green. It was the rancid air around this passenger and the turbulence that put her into a tailspin. He could fix that.

Chopper accepted Felicity's bag from the pilot, who waved to him as he walked back up the dock after locking the plane. Reaching over, he spoke quietly behind her ear as she tried to staunch her gagging. He'd been there.

"Stand over here, baby. Upwind to the dock, downwind to the ocean. Now, just close your eyes and let the sea breeze clear you out." After a couple of minutes, her watery eyes opened, and she was better.

"Thanks. I can normally handle things, but the stink and then the buffeting of the plane was more than I could take."

"Pilot said it was bumpy, but he didn't mention your co-passenger."

"I've smelled rotting, infected flesh, and I never thought there was a smell worse than that, but when that man got on the plane, it was... well, worse." She punctuated her memory with a shiver. "Then the plane kept rolling and hitting air pockets."

"I know. I'm familiar with body funk when someone has been in the field, completing a mission, for way too long. But when I fly them home, if it will take very long, they strip and throw on clean clothes I have because we expect that. The worst of the stink goes into plastic bags to be salvaged later or burned."

"It's horrible. Do you think the man is alright?"

Chopper opened the car door. "Not sure, but I suspect he chooses to live this way."

She nodded. "I've learned people come to Alaska to either be discovered or forgotten. He must be one of the latter."

"I suspect you're right. But you have to be pretty wily and smart to survive this way. I bet he has some cool contraptions at his place."

Felicity laughed. "I'll take your word for it."

Chopper leaned down and kissed her hard. "To be continued. I need to get you home so you can relax. Maybe shower while I grab us dinner. I haven't been back for very long, so no time to pull anything out."

"Mmm, that would be great. Vegetables would be good. I have had plenty of meat this week. Oh, and I have something in my bag for you."

"Yeah? Hold that thought. Watch the door."

He jogged to the driver's side of the SUV and climbed in. He checked to see if she was buckled and slowly pulled off the air company's loading dock. "What are you hungry for?"

"Stir fry would be great. Maybe extra veggies?"

"You got it. Anything else?" Chopper turned to look at Felicity.

"Do we have any ice cream?"

Chopper grinned. "I'll check. Do you see what you did there?" he asked as he pulled into traffic.

"No, what?" she half grinned as though she couldn't help but answer his smile.

"You said 'we.' Do we have any ice cream?"

Felicity shook her head and looked out of the car window. "You're reaching, you know."

"Maybe, but I have hope. So tell me about your week."

Once they arrived home, Chopper hopped out of the car to grab her bag from the back before walking around to meet her at the passenger door she was exiting. He followed in behind her and put down the bag before closing the front car door and locking it. "Did you see what I did there?"

She scrunched up her face. "No." She waited for him to unlock the door to the house before walking inside ahead of him.

"I let you get out of the car yourself without making you wait for me or saying something when you didn't wait. I'd say that was progress."

She chuckled. "If you say so."

"Come here. I missed you the whole long week." Not waiting for an answer, he dropped her bag as his lips touched hers lightly before settling in for the welcome home greeting he had waited to give her. Felicity seemed to melt in his arms, and he tightened his hold to deepen his kiss.

Pulling away to take some deep breaths, Felicity dropped her forehead on his chest and inhaled his masculine, recently showered scent.

"Are you sniffing me, woman?"

"I'd be dead before I didn't notice your scent. Besides, you smell delicious. Which reminds me I need a shower and dinner."

"Okay, but then I want dessert in the bedroom."

"I could be persuaded." Kissing him quickly, Felicity reached down for her bag and headed for the bedroom.

DINNER WAS SATISFYING with fried rice and stir-fried veggies with a side dish of grilled fish. Not precisely an Asian method to cook fish, so he grabbed that at the Seafood Shack before they ran out and closed for the day. Once the fish was gone, it was gone. They only served the fresh catch of the day, and that could be anything from squid, salmon, flounder, and more to abalone or oysters. Whatever came in the door, if it was fresh, it was on the menu.

Today he lucked out, and there were still about three servings of halibut left. He brought it home, threw some seasoning he created especially for white fish, added a small amount of mayo to coat and cracker coating before sliding it into a hot pan of melted butter. He was plating the food when Felicity walked into the kitchen.

"I didn't know just how hungry I was until I smelled this. It looks amazing."

"It does. Sit. I have it all ready."

He pulled out some of Felicity's seaweed stash she liked to eat with a meal like this. Chopper had never cultivated a taste for it outside of sushi, and even then, he ate it because it's what held the rest together. He would have ingested it if necessary in the wild, but he passed it over to others at home.

"This is so good," sighed Felicity when she took a breath from eating.

Chopper chuckled. His girl wasn't one to pretend to eat like a bird. She ate until she was satisfied. Sometimes that was a little bit, and sometimes, like tonight, it was a healthy portion.

"Didn't you eat while you were gone from me?"

She frowned and looked down at her plate. "Well, I did, but eating alone isn't as much fun, and I was so tired, I more made a sandwich and fell into bed. I ate a bigger breakfast."

He reached over and squeezed her hand. "I love that you eat like you enjoy your food. I hate nitpicky ladies who complain about what they are eating, even when they chose it. Or talk about how many calories or how fattening something is, or worse yet, how much they could buy in groceries for the cost of their dinner."

Her eyes grew large. "No one did that. Did they?"

His hand went up as making a vow. "I promise you it has happened to me twice."

"Twice? Boy, does that mean you have bad taste in women?"

He laughed. "Gotta kiss a lot of frogs..."

"No, I have to kiss a lot of frogs. You are part of the army of frogs I have to kiss."

He frowned. "I thought it was a colony."

"Oh, it is. It's Army, Colony or Knot."

"Knot? Are you sure?" His skepticism was unmistakable.

"Promise." She grabbed her phone and proved she was right. "See?"

"Okay, you were right," he nodded. "I don't mind getting in a knot with my army girl."

"Prior Army. I'm a civilian now, remember?" she teased.

"Oh, I remember. I'd love to take you to bed and see if we could get tangled up." He wiggled his eyebrows.

"Later, Casanova. I brought you something." She stood from her chair.

Chopper reached for the empty plates. "I'll clear the table and meet you in the living room."

Felicity nodded and headed to the bedroom. They met in the doorway as she was returning with a small shopping bag. She pushed the gift in his hand. Chopper could see how eager she was for him to open it, so he sat at the end of the sofa and reached inside. He extracted a sealed bag, much like those used with a heat-sealing appliance in the kitchen, he examined the contents.

"Jerky? Looks homemade."

"It is. It's actually several things. Inside the large bag are smoked fish, dried fish, and jerky. I think he said there was caribou, moose and venison and something else, oh, reindeer."

"Who made this sample pack? Looks great."

"One of my patient's family members. They had gone hunting up north, and their meat was packaged at a packing house up there before they brought it back. The deer and fish they got here but caribou and moose from further north. He didn't get a reindeer. He swapped for some at the meat packers. Then he smoked some, froze some, and made jerky with some."

"Thank you. This is great. I plan to go north in the fall to hunt for a moose or something, but right now, this is a treat."

Felicity smiled. "I thought you'd like it. I mean, what guy doesn't like meat?"

"Vegetarians?" he asked facetiously. Then laughed when she did. "There aren't many of those in the truest form in this area. And certainly not me."

"I could give it to someone more deserving."

He pulled Felicity closer and kissed her quickly. "Thank you, and I promise to deserve it." His deeper voice was gravelly, laced heavily with his desire, and her body's response of slight tremors nearly dropped him where he stood. Their next kiss was more profound, more possessive. She whimpered. When they finally separated enough to suck in air, Felicity continued, her voice still wispy and airy from their kiss.

"I thought, if you wanted, you could put one of the packages of dried fish or something in your go-bag, and you'd have protein when you needed it. Within reason, of course."

"It's a great idea." He kissed her again, this time lingering with a touch of passion but not as intense as earlier. "Thank you."

"You know what else is a great idea?" She asked with a touch of sultry sway to her voice.

"What?"

Chopper guessed where Felicity's mind was going, and he wanted to go there with her. He pulled her closer so he could take advantage of her permission when she gave it. She removed the sealed bag of meat from his hand, and he released it without hesitation. His arousal increased as he watched her reach over him to set it on the end table, her now pointy nipples dragging over his chest and dragging back across. She turned to face him.

She put one knee on the sofa cushion and straddled his thighs, planting her other knee on the other side of him. Then she sat on his thighs. After wiggling a few seconds to get comfortable and smiling when he groaned, she wove her fingers in his distinctly non-military regulation hair and leaned down. As she got closer, his staff grew stiffer and uncomfortably swollen. It was sweet torture.

Chopper watched her mouth slowly descend to his, and it was the hottest thing a woman had ever done to him. His hands went up to tangle in her shoulder length hair, and he gripped the strands tightly. The little minx shook her head like he was a naughty boy. Then licked her lips before running her tongue over his. She spoke just a breath's distance from his mouth.

"Uh, uh. I get to be the leader for a while, then you can take over. But it's my turn. Understand, sailor?"

"Yes, ma'am."

His hands fell away. His girl hadn't ever asked to control their play so concisely before. Felicity had been content to let him lead, but he had no objections if she wanted a little bedroom power for a while. She seemed to understand that at some point, he would have to take over. He needed to be in charge, but right now, his beautiful Doc could lead the foreplay, and he would enjoy it.

Bringing her face just that last bit closer to his, she kissed him tenderly at first, but the heat that little touch created brought on a fierce hunger to taste her more intimately. For now, she ran the show, so when she pushed her tongue inside, he readily opened for her. Mimicking the mating dance, he brought her in closer, holding her head as she was holding his.

The passion was rising, and Felicity nearly climbed him, seemingly trying to crawl in his skin. Her hands left his hair to run under his tee-shirt and lift it up. She quickly released his lips to pull his shirt over his head. He leaned forward to make it easier. The second the shirt was tossed to the side, she yanked her top off and reached for his belt while reattaching to his lips.

Hot, furious, almost desperate was his woman. She was becoming impatient, and Chopper vaguely knew his time was near. She'd want it too fast, and in frustration, would give over to him. He was content to wait. She hadn't run the show with him, and her foreplay was a fast fuck. He wanted to give her a good fuck, but building a little anticipation always made the loving better. However, they were both too far gone for his kind of long game, so one orgasm and then a fast fuck it was.

Kissing her back, he placed his hands on her hips and lightly held her steady. Felicity rubbed her center up and down his shaft and moaned as he groaned, both for the same reason: need.

She breathed into his mouth. "Take the jeans off."

"You need to lift up some, baby." He said as he tried to reach between them to unbuckle his belt.

Her sounds of distress made him smile. "Want me to finish this?"

"Hurry."

"Yes, ma'am."

Without another word, Chopper slid his hands under her bottom and heaved forward, lifting her as though she were a part of him and not an awkwardly attached woman. She wrapped her legs around him and held tight. Now it was his head that descended to hers and his lips that took possession.

Bringing them into the bedroom, he dropped her on the bed. As his hands went to his belt, he said, "Strip. Don't make me wait for you. I will punish all dawdling."

His tone deepened, husky with arousal. Naked, he looked up and saw Felicity's scrumptious tits pointing to him, and her pelvis surrounded a well-trimmed muff that caused him to salivate.

"Move back, feet planted on the bed, pussy right here in front of my face."

She huffed her frustration. "No, I need you inside."

He slapped her outer thigh. "I'm in control now, and I know what I'm doing. I promise you will like it." When she wiggled and twisted to get right where he had wanted her, he said, "No moving."

"What? You know that will not happen. I can't be still."

He chuckled. "Do the best you can, woman. I don't want to paddle your ass because you were too antsy to get off."

"No worries there, sir. I will have no trouble... ah... yes, right there. No, ahh, yes, there."

The fleshy slap that resounded when his hand bounced off her thigh brought a squeal. "You are so bad. You got to be boss. Now it's my turn."

Her breathy whimpering sounds nearly did him in. "Hmm, where was I?"

His tongue speared her entrance, following her slit until he came to her clit and circumvented it after teasing the bundle of sensitivity for a few seconds. Sliding back down her channel, stopping to enter her several times before continuing on to her little brown back entrance, he teased its winking, twitching muscle with his tongue before returning via the same route he'd used in his descent.

Her slick arousal was overflowing, and he licked as she wiggled. He held her hips securely to steady her, keeping her anchored to one position. The light restraint seemed to flip her switch even more. Over and over, he licked from clit to anus and back. His own staff becoming diamond hard. He lifted his head slightly, lips glistening before he licked them with sounds of enjoyment.

"Come, baby."

Felicity whimpered. Her labored breathing was the only acknowledgment of Darrell, but it didn't matter because, within a few more swipes of his tongue, she was flooding her valley. He was lapping the river of arousal as Felicity tried hard to bounce out of his ironclad hold. She froze her movements several times, interspersed with renewed efforts at pumping against his face.

Finally, Felicity slowed and then dropped her bottom to the bed. He rose over her and wiped his sweat and arousal covered face on his arm before grabbing her legs in the wheelbarrow hold and plunged inside without further warning.

He would have never taken a woman so suddenly, but it was the way Felicity liked it. He'd discovered that the first time he'd pounded her hard in a round of rough sex. He'd apologized, and she had said it was the best fucking she'd ever had. Chopper wasn't rough all the time, but he made sure he got a session in every so often.

He'd missed her this week, and this urgency felt damn good. She was trying to get him to hit her clit as he went in. He slapped her bare ass twice.

"I told you it was my turn, sweet girl. Don't make me have to redden this backside to get you to behave."

Her only response was a tortured noise like a strangled cry of agony. She was so damn sexy, and Chopper wanted to keep going hard, but he slowed down for their mutual enjoyment. It felt good to rhythmically piston in and out while she grew hotter and her clit grew even fatter, its little head peeking out from its protective hood, taunting him. He took one hand from her hip and let two fingers scoop up some cream, then he teased her button of nerves. Her clit jumped, and she did as well.

"No, don't move, or I'll stop." His harsh grumble drew her pleading.

"Please, please, I'm strung so tight."

"Shh. You're okay. I'll always take care of you, sweetheart."

And he meant it in more than sex. Felicity was his. Her little sounds of distress as she tried to do as he asked were fucking cute. He had to take her into orbit with him right now, or she would shoot off without him. He picked up the pace and placed his right-hand forefinger on her clit, his thumb on the other hand between their bodies on her anus, and pressed. Chopper didn't stop until his thumb had penetrated, and she had shouted as she came. He was so primed, he followed in two pumps. His own grunt of release was long.

It wasn't until several moments later that he remembered she was out of pills. He was momentarily worried, but then it left. It was an automatic reaction of fear, born from many years of being careful, not something he really felt tonight. He had many one-night stands and several exclusive girlfriends but never engaged in sex of any kind that was unprotected until Felicity. She was clean and on the pill. They usually barebacked, but now the implications were clear. Dammit.

She had rolled onto the bed further and reached for him. He put his hand out to hers and grasped tight. "Felicity, baby. Did you happen to get your pills refilled this week?"

"What—" her eye grew huge. "Darrell, I... no. I didn't. I forgot. Of all the stupid things to forget." She was quiet for a moment and then looked at him. "I'm sorry. I really did forget. This wasn't on purpose."

His face held a puzzled look. "I know that, honey. I wouldn't have thought it was. Look, I'll use a condom from now on until you're comfortable you're protected again. Go to sleep, you're tired."

Felicity was quiet for a little while as she snuggled close to him. He lay awake, wondering how they would handle it if their accident became more than that. Chopper wanted a family and knew he needed to get a move on, but he'd just decided that Felicity was for him. Hell, he hadn't even started his business yet. And yes, he was going into business for himself. For him, it was right.

She wiggled and repositioned herself the way she did to sleep. She wiggled in closer to his body and drew his arm around her. Then she slipped her ankle between his and wiggled her butt. He leaned over to kiss her cheek and pulled her tightly to him. Her little sigh said she was ready to sleep and was entirely unconcerned with the implications of their slip-up tonight. It took a little longer for Chopper to find his sleep.

Laying with her, breathing on her neck, wanting to wake her and have her again, he shifted his thinking. Content in the knowledge that if Felicity was that fertile, and he was that potent that one time did it, he was fucking okay with that, but he didn't want to do something purposely that she might not be in agreement over. She'd said several times she wanted children someday soon. But this might not have been as soon as she was thinking.

He hadn't even told her he had fallen in love with her. Now, if he offered to marry her, would she do the now well-used phrase, "how do I know you really love me, and it isn't just the baby?"

Chopper, man, don't get ahead of yourself. But he wasn't. He would declare himself soon so that if something did come of this oops, she would be confident that he loved her. No question. But it saddened him to acknowledge that she wasn't likely pregnant after one time. He wanted a child with Felicity. Hell, he wanted all his children with her.

He would set out to show her she meant everything to him, and he wanted all his tomorrows with her. All he could hope for was that she was emotionally going in the way he had already gone and wouldn't be put off by his declaration of feelings toward her. Darrell fell asleep with his arm over Felicity's back as she was now sleeping on her belly. He tossed one leg over her thighs, thinking of his tactical maneuvers necessary to gain her agreement that they were good together. Because they were.

Chapter 9

Felicity, just partially awake, grinned when she climbed on top of Darrell's nocturnal aroused cock. She'd woken up to the early high school chant of "tab A into slot B" running through her head. Felicity was a little sore, but she only felt a twinge when she slid over his cock and then gently settled him inside, making sure she fully seated herself.

When she heard him stop his soft snore, she knew he was awake. She suspected he had been awake for the whole process, but he was kind enough not to take over when she wanted to do this herself. Up and down, slowly and gently, her eyes closed to revel in the experience. She moaned quietly when two hands suddenly massaged her breasts.

She was more aroused the longer he caressed her. Her movements became more urgent, her lubrication more copious. She wanted to have children with Darrell, but she was a doctor and a responsible person. They would have to have a conversation. But not now. Right now, she needed this intimacy. No words, no sounds, just pre-dawn coitus. Sweet connection, simple loving. And she did love him. Felicity didn't know what Darrell thought of their relationship, but she was lost in him.

He took over, holding her hips and moving his own pelvis to increase her need to come. She could feel her core tighten, her anus was clenching, and her inner muscles began an undulation that helped its ache. She reached down and touched herself. It was heaven. She manipulated her clit just the way she liked it, increasing the tension in her body and feeling her lover's movements become more frenzied.

Felicity sat up straighter and braced her knees further apart for balance. She then put her hand on her breast and increased the pressure on her clit, squeezing and twisting her nipple the way she liked. Not as good as when Darrell played, but good enough. When the wave of orgasm swept over her, she heard her man say, "thank God," before he took over. She smiled and braced on his sculpted chest as he, too, was swept away on the explosive culmination of his release.

He rolled her off his fast-deflating cock and cuddled her close, their combined release freely flowing out of her. It was messy and a second significant event, but she was ready for the result. She hoped he was as well.

HE KNEW WHAT HE HAD done, and there were no avenues to retrace their steps. That Chopper had not stopped her from going another round without protection early this morning was proof that he wanted a baby with her but not that he wanted her. He had to stop this shit until they had an understanding.

He wanted her, the family, the relationship, everything, but now it might not matter whether or not they wanted to travel this avenue; they had begun. It was time to make sure she knew he was good with it and them and believed it. There would be no doing things on her own. If they made a child together, they raised the child together. He'd grown up with the single-parent experience, and it wouldn't happen for his own if he could help it. And he could.

The second round of unprotected sex wasn't just an accident, it was deliberate. Felicity knew what she was doing as much as he did. She declared her intent, and he agreed by allowing it. He needed a commitment. He had to tighten his flight plan, get tactical, maybe call in the strategist and the team leader to see what they thought. Hell, he might even rope in Ryder on the phone. Yeah, he'd call the guys and see if they could meet today.

FELICITY COULDN'T BELIEVE that she had not one but two rounds of unprotected sex, especially during her fertile time. What was wrong with her? She always followed the rules. She did what she needed to do but performed all within Standard Operating Procedures and did not drop the responsibility ball, ever. So what had gotten into her, and why wasn't she freaked out that she might have done the one thing she wanted, but after marriage.

Maybe because Felicity was sure of her feelings concerning Darrell. She loved him. She wanted to spend her life with him. The rush of hot emotion, whenever she looked at him or thought of him, wasn't the first blush of lust. It went deeper than that, so much deeper. She wanted children with him, a home with him, she wanted him. But how to let him know without making it seem she was aggressive?

It was one thing to form a relationship with a person, but to create life was a whole other level of commitment not everyone wanted to take. She didn't want to trap him, and they had not talked about forever, well, not in a personal commitment sort of way. She wouldn't want to raise a child alone. Felicity needed to give her children the security that she was raised with. She'd do what she had to do, but she'd rather do it together.

Felicity was confused, and she needed reinforcements. It was time for a little female bonding. She picked up her phone while Darrell was in the shower.

Alli Wellesley answered the phone. "Felicity? Is everything alright?"

"Yes, physically, I'm fine. But I need a little advice. Do you think you could carve some time out for me today?"

"Hold on, let me pull out the calendar. You are definitely in luck. I don't carpool for the soccer game today, so I'm free from Noon until three. Will that be enough time? If not, I'll call the sitter."

"Maybe? I thought I'd call Kayla too, and maybe even see if Jenn was available."

"Whoa, it must be something big. I'll get a sitter. You make your calls, and I'll meet you at the Café at noon. Well, give me time to come to you, but it shouldn't be more than fifteen minutes or so."

"Thank you. See you then."

By the time Darrell was done in the shower, Felicity had made her calls and cooked breakfast. Kayla was going to take some pictures today, but the weather turned, so she was free.

"Not that I wouldn't have put it off for a friend anyway, but it was convenient that I wasn't doing anything. River got a call earlier, and he has to go out for a few hours, so I don't even have to beg off from him. You've got timing."

When Jenn answered the phone, she sounded like she hadn't been up very long. Why would she? After amicably breaking up with her boyfriend Kendall last summer, she didn't have much to do in her off-hours. She'd come back a few months ago, and since she didn't have the café to run, she'd been substitute teaching at the elementary school.

"Wow, it must be pretty big to call all of us in for a pow-wow."

Felicity hesitated. "It might be. I just need some bonding. You in?"

"You bet I'm in. At the café?"

"Yes, if that's alright. Would it be better at another place?"

"It's fine. In fact, it works out well. I have to talk to you all about some things too. When?"

"At about noon or a few minutes after?"

"Got it. I'll make sure we have a place to sit in the back corner. See you there."

Felicity sighed in relief. If this little group of friends couldn't figure everything out, no one could. She'd never had friends, well, not in this way, and when she agreed to give a presentation to Alli's students soon after she'd arrived, that cinched their friendship. They had gone to lunch afterward and found such a common ground that when Alli began dating Zed, Felicity was there with her. Felicity knew that if she'd been less wrapped up in her job, she would have met Darrell earlier, and things might have taken a whole new direction.

WALKING INTO THE CAFÉ, Felicity couldn't believe her good luck. She didn't have to explain herself or anything when she got ready to go because Darrell had already gone to some strategy meeting with the guys. She guessed they were working or looking at the feasibility of a mission for Zed's group or Kayla's family.

Felicity knew what River Bennett and Zed Wellesley did in the military before River got out, and Zed moved here to create the training center. She knew they had another friend, Ryder Mason, who was in San Diego and was now a paper pusher for Zed. Sort of.

River now worked for his family's foundation attached to their engineering firm, and he and Kayla planned to get married at some point. River worked with Kayla's father's group occasionally and with Zed's trainees to round out the numbers sometimes. Also, he was on the search and rescue when they needed him with Darrell, but daily he ran his family's foundation.

They were a busy bunch of men, but the community and the world were better for what they'd done and still did. They were contributors, and Felicity was proud to be a part of their group. Darrell said he'd be back in time for dinner. She had all afternoon, but the others had other obligations, so she needed to state the issue and then let them all talk about it. They needed their own tactical plan for this situation. Maybe she should have called the strategists instead of their women. But she needed her friends for that all-important bonding. Men wouldn't understand.

Kayla was already at the table when Felicity arrived, and Jenn had just walked in. Within ten minutes, Alli was tripping through the door. Literally. All the women jumped up to get to her, but a big, strapping logger grabbed her before she went down and held her steady until she smiled and nodded. She was good. The ladies walked with her to the table.

"If you got hurt because I needed to talk, I would have been horrified. Alli, please be careful."

Alli gave them a half grimace laced with a smile. "Please don't tell Zed. I am already going crazy with his over-protectiveness. These guys are out of control when it comes to their wives."

"And girlfriends," added Kayla.

"I'm finding Darrell is okay with me, but I'm not...," Felicity hesitated, then pointed to Alli's belly and shrugged. "He is a little overprotective at times, but not much." The lame ending to her statement made her friends pause, but thankfully, no one called her out on it.

Kayla turned to Jenn. "And I think it's time we find you a protective man."

"No, thank you. I don't think I have the constitution for it. I mean, I love your guys, but I don't have the patience to deal with a bossy man."

"So that's what you need to deal with them. No wonder I wanted to clobber River yesterday. Did you know what that man did? The UPS guy came to the door, and he wouldn't let me answer it."

"I thought you had an electronic gate," said Alli.

"Not here. But in Seattle, yes."

"He was protecting you," said Jenn.

"Not buying it," said Alli. "Our UPS guy went to school with River, I think."

"Yep. Some days the man gets on my nerves." Kayla gave them a crooked smile. "But I love him."

"I get it. I didn't think I was going to be able to handle Zed, either." Alli looked around. "I don't think any of us were ready for what we got but wouldn't give them up for anything. Anyway, let's order lunch. I'm starving. Then we'll find out what Felicity needs to talk about."

The women, in unison, pointedly looked at Felicity, and even though she was rarely intimidated, this was a delicate subject, and she could feel the heat rise to her cheeks. The little group was enjoying more good-natured banter when their lunch was served. They all looked at Alli's plate overflowing with food and a bowl of salad. Kayla and Jenn's eyes grew large, but Felicity knew a pregnant woman's appetite was a fickle thing.

"Now, please tell Zed about this." Alli indicated the food. "He says I don't eat enough. He just remembers the times I'm not hungry more than he remembers times like this." She grinned and cut into her first bite of chicken.

Kayla smiled. "I'll log it in the memory banks and pull it out when you need saving. Better yet, I'll take a picture of the plate and your full mouth!" Alli nodded and gave her a thumbs up for photographic history, and continued to eat. "I'll just send to Zed. There. Done."

A response text from Zed arrived quickly. "Take a picture of the empty plate," it read.

Kayla shared his text, and the women laughed. Alli smiled, her mouth full. She nodded in Felicity's direction. Felicity put down her fork.

"Okay, so how do you know if the guy you have is the one for you? I mean, I know what I feel, and it's confusion."

"You like Chopper, right?" asked Jenn. "I mean, the man is a golden god."

"More than like him. But my biological clock is ticking, and my desire to have children is becoming a little pressured. Physically I can wait a little longer, but emotionally, I'm really ready to take the plunge." The women ate in silence for a bit before continuing.

"What does Chopper say about it?" asked Kayla.

"We haven't really talked specifically about us co-parenting yet."

"Don't you think that would have been your best choice? I mean, do you want children with Chopper?" asked Alli.

"Yes. I want everything with him."

Jenn spoke and nodded her head. "But you don't know if he is ready to be a dad or make babies with you."

"Yes and no. I mean, he seems like he does."

The women ate in silence for a few more bites. "You know," said Kayla, "River and I settled things between ourselves before we talked about children."

Alli nodded. "Zed and I were committed before we made our little jelly-bean here. Maybe you need to settle how you feel about each other before you decide the next step."

"But shouldn't I get his thinking on having children with me first? I mean, in case he doesn't want children at this time of his life."

Jenn huffed a laugh. "How old is he? I'd have said mid-thirties."

"He turned forty-two this year," said Felicity. "But you know age and having children hold a different meaning for men and women. I need to get going if I want to have any space between children and enjoy the pregnancy."

"So, what is holding you back from telling him? Why haven't you had this conversation with him?" asked Kayla.

"Honestly? I don't know."

Alli asked, "Why is this suddenly, now, such an important question?" The woman was astute.

"Because I may have had unprotected sex last night."

"Oh," said Jenn. "May have had, or had?"

"Had."

Alli nodded. "Well, I understand your concern, but as a doctor, you know once is often not enough."

Felicity sighed. "And this morning."

"Gotcha," said Kayla with a nod.

"And I'm ovulating," added Felicity.

Jenn let out a low whistle. "Holy cannoli, girl."

"Exactly," agreed Felicity. She leaned back in her chair.

"Well, isn't this all a moot point then?" asked Alli.

"What? No. I just need to deal with this possibility, our feelings, and where we are in our relationship. It is delicate, and I figure you girls have dealt with sensitive issues in your relationships. I've rarely had an exclusive boyfriend."

Alli shook her head and pinned Felicity with a confused look. "You're a person who gets to the heart of the issue and then deals with it. Your confidence amazes me sometimes. I've learned that about you. So what is the problem here?"

"This is a place I've never been before, and you all, or most of you have. I don't want to screw it up. It's too important."

"Okay, so what has Chopper said about this whole thing? I mean, he definitely knows you had unprotected—"

"Oh, yes, he does. Nothing gets by that man. He pointed it out last night. Last week, before I left to work off-island, he said he wanted us to live together. I balked. He said I needed to tell people we were together, but my relationships start folding when I moved forward, looking for something more. It's complicated but hard for me to allow that last final push for permanency."

Jenn was reflective. "And yet, you did something much more than move in that direction. You took a nosedive into the pool of commitment. You could be pregnant."

"Well, not technically. It takes longer than a few hours," laughed Felicity. "But yes, you're right."

Kayla nodded. "Humor. You'll need that dealing with Chopper. And newsflash. That man would not have risked you becoming pregnant if he wasn't on board."

Alli finished her lunch with a big sigh. "You're ready for that next step. You aren't freaking out about the pseudo-accident. You're worried about Chopper's reception. I agree with Kayla. He has already claimed you, or we wouldn't be having this particular conversation. Hell, he had already claimed you when you were at our barbeque."

"You're right about Chopper and probably about me too. I think I am ready. It's just such a big step, moving in, being exclusive, having babies. I mean, I want it, but what if it falls apart? I'm terrified of that."

"We all are to a degree but talk openly and do the best you can. That's all anyone can ask for. You'll get past the part about worried if it's going to last and move on to... buying a house, opening your practice, having babies."

Felicity shook her head and laughed. "One thing at a time, please."

Jenn leaned back. "I really love these guys, and I said when I met Chopper, he was something fine. Except for that over-possessive, Me Tarzan, You Jane kind of thing, he was worth a second look. I'm looking for someone who doesn't get all macho over things."

"I remember when I thought that way. Remember, I have two older brothers and a retired military father. Testosterone was heavy around my house. But when it is directed at you in a lover kind of way," Kayla sighed, "There is nothing better."

"Okay, you've given me lots to think about, ladies, and some sound advice. Let's not waste our time on my need to talk to Chopper, so what else is going on?"

Jenn cleared her throat. "So I have an announcement. I think I'm going to open a business, well, buy into one, anyway."

The women jumped on that information and gave Felicity a moment to think about how she would proceed. She just needed to choreograph it the way she wanted without making a mess of everything. Darrell was an incredible man that would want his way often. She knew that but instinctively also knew that the type of man he'd shown himself to be would be present more intensely for the woman he loved. She hoped she was that woman.

"WOMEN ARE DAMNED DIFFICULT to steer," said Chopper as he picked up his club sandwich to take a big bite.

Zed laughed. "Well, that's because they aren't one of your planes."

"I assume by women, you mean Felicity," said River as he cut into his steak sandwich.

He nodded and finished chewing. "Yes. But I do mean women in general, too. But today, most specifically Felicity."

Ryder spoke to them through Zed's phone. Zed got a text, switched over to it, laughed and shared the picture of Alli's plate loaded with food that Kayla sent to him. He texted a response, then switched back to Ryder. "Sorry, man, had to take care of that."

"No worries, now I don't have much time to have a girlie chit chat, but I wanted to weigh in. So what's the deal, Chopper? Having woman problems?"

"It's Felicity. I asked her to move in with me, and she explained that when she gets deeper in a relationship, they always fall apart because she is terrified of commitment or doing it wrong, so she sabotages the bond instead of building it stronger. My words partly, not hers. She pushes people away, her love interests, so they don't get too close. Then the men go the other way after a while because she closes them out. She doesn't want to do that with us."

Ryker said, "So don't let her. Call her on it every time she puts up a barrier. Push at it, so it doesn't have a chance to stay erect."

Zed laughed. "Ryker, that's good advice. Why aren't you married?"

"Because I'm smarter than the average man, and my dick hasn't taken over my brain."

"Yet," said Hunter.

"I'm not marriage material. Besides, no woman wants a man who has only had the Navy as his mistress, who's graying around the temples, and bossy as hell."

Chopper spoke. "Silver foxes are all the rage."

"I haven't found her yet, then. Okay, gotta meeting of equal importance in the other room, and since the Navy pays me, I need to leave you knuckleheads to figure out Chopper's woman. I look forward to meeting all your women. I might need to take a trip north soon."

"Do," said Zed. "But wait until the baby is born."

"I'll see what I can do about that. Over and out."

"Out, here." Zed put his phone away and looked back to Chopper. "Now, what you need is to get her to admit her feelings for you. Have you declared yours?"

"Not completely. I mean, I asked Felicity to move in with me or me with her. Just together."

River grinned. "Not enough, man. She has to hear the words. Women do not jump to the next logical step before having the last step clearly marked. They don't want to make a mistake."

"Assumptions are bad," agreed Zed.

"Okay, so I declare my feelings, inquire about hers, then get her to move in."

Zed shook his head. "No, you need exclusivity."

"I think we already have that," said Chopper dryly.

"You think, or you know? This is a mission, and you have to know all your steps beforehand. Otherwise, instead of arriving at your destination with your target alive, you both end up as blown-up bits on the side of the road."

"Great. Thanks for that analogy," said Chopper shaking his head and grinning.

River leaned in with his forearms on the table. "Right, so here it is. You sneak in under her radar, take her by surprise, get her to safety, love her good, tell her you think it's time to up the stakes, then don't take no for an answer."

"And how did that work for you, River?" asked Zed.

"Kayla slipped in an IED before I had a chance to take cover. But we're good now." The men chuckled.

"Right, well, we have one further possible complication on the horizon." The men stared at Chopper.

"Shit, man, are you kidding me? You know how to suit up. You're no rookie." River leaned back in his chair and folded his arms over his chest. His countenance, severe.

"Well, that does add to the level of urgency," said Zed as he, too, leaned back.

"We don't know. It just happened last night." Chopper paused. "And this morning."

"Hell, you might as well go buy a ring, too. You ready for that possibility?"

"Hell yeah, I'm ready. I had no idea it would happen, but I'm ready for it. I don't want Felicity to believe I want her because of this possible event, though. That isn't me."

Zed shook his head. "She won't because you asked her to move in a week ago. Two separate events. You have already staked your claim and made the first move. She simply has to trust you to be who she needs."

"And trust herself more than she has in past relationships to make this good." River checked the time. "Okay, I've had enough male bonding. You'll do fine if you just tell it like it is. You want her, she wants you, and you want it together. Now, let me tell you about my window shopping trip in Paraguay."

"Yeah," said Chopper, "what was that all about? Is Kayla looking to do a story or shoot there?" Zed asked.

"Over my dead body."

Chapter 10

Felicity had gone into the office for a few hours after leaving her friends to try and get some paperwork prepped for Monday. Being gone a week always made the following Monday packed. She checked her appointment calendar and grimaced. She was booked Monday and Tuesday, but then things leveled out by Wednesday afternoon. Not too bad, really.

She stopped and bought dinner, then texted Chopper. She didn't know if he would be home yet, but he would be hungry whenever he got there. Home. Yes, she examined that statement, and it didn't give her the same trapped feeling it had the only other time a man suggested they move in together. A good sign.

Felicity: "Bought dinner."

Chopper: "Hell. I did too."

Felicity: "That's okay. It might be a long night."

There was no Chopper response, and she tried not to read anything into that except that he was a man. A hot, sexy, take-charge man that she prayed she was able to keep in her life. Might as well start now.

When she arrived home, he was already there, and Felicity wondered how he had gotten into the house. She'd locked the front door and was home whenever he had come by before. Chopper greeted her as she walked up the steps, and after taking the bag from her and following her into the house, he set the bag on the counter, looking for silverware.

"How did you get in? I locked the front door." She asked as she grabbed the glasses.

"You did. However, you did not lock the back door." No missing the displeased tones of her protector.

"It was locked. You checked last night." Good defense.

"And you threw dry bread out to the deer and birds this morning."

Silence.

"Oh."

"Felicity, you have got to pay attention to your surroundings. I know there are fewer crimes than in most areas, but there is crime. And someone has to be the victim of that crime, and it won't be you by your own hand. Not if I have anything to say about it."

"I'm sorry. You're right."

"Honey, you have to be careful and don't be sorry, be informed."

She tried hard not to laugh, but she couldn't hold it in. "I promise." She laughed again, and Darrell smiled.

"Okay, what's so funny, woman."

"You sounded like one of those neighborhood watch commercials." She spoke with a fake deep voice. "Don't be sorry, be informed."

He grinned wider and pulled Felicity tight to him. He swatted her ass once, right in the center, hard enough that she felt the sting and her butt cheeks jiggled.

"Ow!"

"You can be so naughty sometimes." His hand went up to move the segment of hair behind her ear. "I missed you this afternoon."

Their lips pressed hard together. Darrell took the kiss deeper before pulling back and laying his forehead against hers.

"I missed you too." She took a deep breath. "We need to talk."

He hesitated and then nodded firmly as he stepped back from her. "We do. I'm starving, so I'm glad you had the same idea I did because I'm not sure I got enough to meet my appetite."

"You're always hungry."

"Listen, woman. You usually feed me by this time of the evening. I'm a man of routine."

"I guess you're right. Then eat until you're full. I bought meatloaf and mashed potatoes, your comfort food, from the deli."

Darrell laughed. "Funny, I bought enchiladas and rice from the deli for you."

"Perfect. You take what I bought, and I'll take what you bought. Then you can have what I don't eat from my meal. Good for you?"

"I like the way you think, Doc."

"Okay, other people call me Doc, especially Zed and his crew, but try to refrain. I call you Darrell so you can call me Felicity."

"All the time?"

"Most of the time."

"I can do that." He moved in close. "But what about honey," he kissed her cheek. "Sugar." He kissed the other one. "Or maybe, Sweetheart?" he kissed her lips again.

When he lifted his head, she smiled. "I can handle that."

"Good. Now let's eat." Darrell picked up the food and began to take it to the dining table.

"And talk," added Felicity.

He looked at her for a moment. "And talk."

After five solid minutes of Darrell eating, he leaned back. "I'm not going to starve now."

"Wow. You've finished already?" asked Felicity as she looked at his empty plate.

"Not finished, just out of the danger zone."

"You eat a lot. Like Rex, the Newfoundland dog my father had. He was always hungry, strong as an ox, and loved the water. If you were in the Navy, you must at least like the water."

"I can see I should have swatted that cute little ass a few more times earlier."

"No, you should not have. I was just making a comparison. A very appropriate one, actually."

"Okay, baby," his countenance sobered, "We need to talk."

"I know. Maybe after we finish eating?"

"We'll eat, but we need to start. No more avoidance. I'll go first. I haven't told you in words because it wasn't until you were about to leave this time for the island that I realized how much I really want you in my life. Forever. Asking you to move in together was a guy's very inadequate way of telling you how much I want you."

There wasn't an inkling of indecision or lack of confidence in this man. He knew where he was going, and it gave her the needed reassurance to respond with her heart and head. She reached her hand out to him, weaving their fingers.

"I love you feel like that about me, but I'm still worried that I'll push you away."

"I understand that's who you were with others, but I think, no, I know that because I have a heads up, I won't allow that to happen. We will both be on the lookout for it. Expect me to stop any behaviors that go in that direction." His set jaw and lifted eyebrow left her with no misunderstanding. He meant it.

"I believe you." She looked at him with a clear, steady gaze.

"Good. Then you understand I'm going to call you on things when you are obviously or subtly trying to put space between us."

"I don't know about that. I have my own opinions and like to be heard," her voice a little militant. "And I don't like to be told what to do. I left the Army for a reason."

"And it wasn't that reason. Did I say anything about not listening to you or disrespecting you?" his tone was reasonable and earnest.

Felicity looked at the empty plate she scrapped with her fork. "No."

He placed his crooked finger under her chin and lifted. "See, just like that, you were trying to cause a rift, but I'm not letting you." He stood and leaned over to kiss her forehead. "Good, that's settled. But we're not finished talking. You done here?" he nodded at the remnants of dinner.

She held up the majority of the enchilada plate. "I can't eat any more of this, but it's a good leftover."

He laughed. "I wouldn't know what makes good leftovers since I rarely have them. You take care of the leftovers, and I'll clean the table. Okay?" Felicity nodded.

Darrell didn't mean to take over the conversation, but he had an agenda and intended to get through it before they made love tonight, and he intended on that as well.

After the kitchen was taken care of, they ended on the sofa. Darrell wanted her in his lap but knew it put an unfair advantage in his court. Nothing was going to be said that would make her think she was outmaneuvered. Felicity sat sideways on the sofa, legs crossed. He shook his head. He hadn't been able to fold his body in that way in over twenty years. Working his muscles to a descent bulk negated that ability.

"I prefer you closer, but maybe this is a good way to get through the discussion and on to things I want to do... to you."

"Oh, yeah?" Her face pinkened, and she gave him a shy smile. His pants were tight already.

"Yeah, so help me out here. I'm ready to share my days and nights with you permanently. I hope you're ready for that." Felicity opened her mouth, but Darrell held up his hand. "Me, first. But I won't pressure you or make you decide tonight. I will say that I am falling in love with you, and it is the next natural step for me. We are more than grown. We have goals and are looking at timetables to mesh those. So, with that in mind, I want to share my life with you, starting now."

He reached for her hands that lay in her lap and held them lightly. When she tried to pull them back, he tightened his grip. Felicity relaxed.

"My turn?" Felicity asked. Darrell nodded. "Okay. I'm so into you that I'm lost when we don't see each other every day. And that scares me, but I'm trusting you to make it okay for me, for us. I'm willing to compromise. Where do you want to live? My place or yours?"

Darrell smiled and kissed her hands. He showed his excitement. "Actually? Neither. You know the house in the cul-de-sac that Zed and Alli live on that has three houses?" She nodded. "The third house is up for sale. The one closest to the beach. It has five acres of forest behind it, undeveloped, and I just need about an acre to make my office and hangar. I may want to start my own business if you want to stay here, but I won't if you think you want to move."

"I've been thinking about doing my own practice, but I don't think I really want to do that huge undertaking right now, if ever. I have security, and I might need it if we..., you start your own business. Besides, I would need a business manager, a receptionist and Alli. And courage. Alii won't be available for some time, so I want to put that on the back burner. I think this community would be a wonderful place to raise... a wonderful place to live."

"And raise children. Our children. That's where I'm leaning, but until you can commit, we will not have unprotected sex again. It may be too late, but if it isn't, then we aren't tempting fate again without your agreement."

"How do we buy a house, open a business, and have children at the same time? We can't. We'll need stability." Her worry was settling over her like a wet wool blanket.

"I have a plan I've been working on, and I know I can get plenty of customers. That's my side of things. You need to say yes to at least staying with me.

Trust me. I'll talk to you every step of the way. Time to prove you trust me." He lifted his eyebrows and smiled his encouragement. She gave him a timid smile in return. "Felicity."

She tingled at that masterful way he had but grimaced. "Okay. I trust you, so see what you can figure out." Chopper swooped her up in his arms. "Darrell, put me down!"

"When will you move into my place?"

"But mine's bigger."

"Okay, tell you what. I'll sleep here on the weekdays, and you come to me on the weekends. When we buy the house, we move in together. When is your lease up?"

"Three months. Yours?"

"Five. So if we don't have it done in time, you can store your things and move in with me for the last bit. If it is, I already have someone ready to take over my lease."

The kiss they shared was intense, happy, relieved. Felicity was more receptive than she usually was to change. She wasn't carrying the burden of decisions alone and making all the choices for the next steps in her life. Felicity was going to take those steps with someone. She pushed back the worry that something would stop all their beginning walk to their forever. Not this time, she vowed.

TWO WEEKS LATER, FELICITY'S cell phone rang just after six a.m. "Hello?"

She wasn't on call, so she couldn't imagine who would call her at this hour of the morning, on the weekend. Darrell lifted up, immediately alert. She wished she could do that as well as he could. He fell asleep at the drop of a hat, too. "Who is this? Oh, right. Where is Doctor Maggiano?"

"I see. Wouldn't it be better to get him? He's the one who monitors that patient ongoing." She listened to the response and sighed. "I see. Are you sure you don't just want to medivac him?" Felicity nodded and looked at Darrell, frowned and shook her head. "Fine. I'll get over there as soon as I can." She hung up.

"What's going on?"

"It's a patient on Watchers Island. I have to check on a patient. He won't come over here for anything. I've heard he hasn't left the island for more years than people can remember."

"You aren't supposed to go until Monday."

"I know," she said as she crawled out of the warm covers and walked to the bathroom. "The resident doctor is off getting married in Seattle. So, no such luck getting him to do it."

"Good luck to him. I wish you'd think about—"

"I can't hear you. Hey," Felicity leaned out of the bathroom doorway, "can you call the flights to see when the next one with an available seat is? It's short notice, and there might not be any."

"I'll take you over. Just grab your gear. It'll have to be my helicopter because I wasn't going to take any flights today since you were home."

"No, you do what you need to do. I'll just wait for a seat."

"Your patient might not be able to wait."

She walked back into the bedroom, biting her bottom lip. "You might be right."

"I am."

"I'll just stay until I come home at the end of the week. Maybe I can come back Friday morning rather than the afternoon."

"Okay, if you want to. Otherwise, I can hang around and bring you back. Same trip."

She thought a moment. "Nah, I'll just start today instead of Monday and get done faster. Maybe even Thursday if people are accommodating."

"Are you sure?"

She nodded. "I am."

"I'll go make you breakfast."

"Just coffee."

"With breakfast." When Chopper was adamant like that, it was easier to give in early. "Okay." He smiled, kissed her gently, and grabbed boxers on his way out of the room.

"But, what if I get sick?" Her concern was loud and clear.

"Are you feeling sick?" He stuck his head back in the bedroom. His face showed concern.

"No."

"Then stop trying to take charge. I'll do breakfast, and you get ready."

"I guess I don't want to leave yet."

She watched him stride back into the bedroom, pull her from rummaging in the closet, and kissed her hard. "Me either, but then we get a long weekend next week, right?"

"Mmm, that could work in our favor."

"It could. It definitely could."

"Okay, I'll put the discontent away. I haven't had anyone I wanted to linger with as much as you."

"Compliment accepted and returned. Now hop to it, woman." He slapped her butt, and she laughed.

Within a little over two hours, they were preparing to land. "Chopper?"

"Hmm?"

"I'm going to test this week for pregnancy. I don't think I am, but just so we can go on. Once I know, I can start back on the pill with a negative result and go on as we have been."

"No, don't start them again. I'll just suit up for now. You said it was optimal to be off for at least a month so, it's been two weeks now. That way, when we're ready, you don't have those hormones in your body. Besides, I don't like the idea of doing that to your system. There have to be better methods."

"There are, but we don't have time to talk about my thoughts on them. Maybe next weekend."

"Sounds good. Landing."

CHOPPER STAYED AROUND for several hours to make sure everything was okay before taking off again. He rode with Felicity to the clinic, and then they took the man home in the clinic vehicle. She promised to check back before she ended her day. She fit two more patients in before saying goodbye.

His gut just wasn't good with this. Something felt off, but nothing looked wrong. Even the patient who had initiated her early arrival appeared to have resolved by the time she arrived.

"Don't forget I want dinner on Friday. It's your night to cook."

"Take out it is."

His kiss was hungry with a hint of desperation, and it had been hard to let her go. She gave him a perplexed look before waving him off. It was going to be a rough week. Chopper spoke to Felicity every night, but his gut didn't relax. Especially after his last conversation with her.

"So, how has your day gone?" Chopper asked.

"Really good, actually."

"But? I hear something in your voice."

"Oh, it's nothing, I just... Well, there has been a lot of talk over here this week about a couple of incidents that bother me a little."

Chopper was instantly alert. "Tell me."

She sighed. "It's probably nothing but... well, okay. One of my patients, a retired Forest Service Ranger, was talking to his neighbor. I just listened in while they finished their chat. The neighbor said a male, late forties, maybe early fifties, tried to take a woman right off the main road at dusk. She yelled, but apparently, no one heard her. She was able to get away and get a ride home the next morning, early."

Chopper was pacing by then. "Did the police catch him?"

"No. But he might not even exist."

"Explain."

"My patient said his neighbor was friendly, but she believed everything she heard. He hadn't been in town recently, but he expected he would have heard about it if it was true."

"Did you check it out?"

"Well, that's just it. The young lady in question has evidently stayed out all night before, and it was something she would say to get out of trouble. My patient figured she was getting desperate for a new story. It was much more likely that she'd stayed out with her boyfriend."

"What do you think, baby?"

"Well, this is a big island with lots of people living off the grid. I have heard whispers of missing women or teens being called to babysit or what have you and disappearing over the years, but I have never been able to find someone to corroborate the stories. Sounds like old westerns rather than modern-day island life. I haven't ever given it more than a passing thought."

"But this bothers you. I can hear it in your voice." His concern was as loud to her as hers was to him.

"It does, a little." She hesitated before continuing. "I'm just tired. Things like this don't normally bother me."

"My point. I'm flying over to get you." His deep, confident voice brooked no argument and yet she argued.

"No, I'm home tomorrow evening. Don't you dare waste time and gas to come over. I'm fine. Really fine."

Against his better judgment, he allowed her to convince him she was coming home the next day and was safe. He rarely allowed anyone to change his mind when he felt, on a visceral level, that he needed to do something. However, Felicity was sharp as a tack and well trained in her field and better prepared in the fieldwork than most. He had to trust her instincts no matter how much it went against his concerns. He would just pick her up from her flight over and baby her.

But come Thursday, there was a search and rescue job he was asked in on. He tried calling Felicity, but it went to voice mail. She was likely busy or out of range. He sent a text and hoped she'd read it before climbing on the plane if she was coming back today. She would need to take a cab, and he wanted her to know that.

It bothered him his plans were changed again, but he had learned long ago to roll with the punches and the schedule changes. He had a twinge of raw gut, but that was likely because he expected a grueling night in search of missing kids. He hated these rescues, and yet, they happened all too often.

Felicity missed Darrell something awful. She would do the pregnancy test this afternoon and wanted him on the phone when she got the results, but she figured he was flying when she couldn't get a call to go through to him.

Felicity decided to have the technician put the results in an envelope and seal it. She would bring it home, and they would open it together. It had taken almost the entire two weeks since they had unprotected sex for Felicity to come to terms with the fact that she loved Darrell, and she loved they were building a life together. That little envelope would tell them how fast that life was going to expand to three.

Chapter 11

Chopper was dragging ass when he got back home. It was almost three a.m., and the outcome had not been all good. They found the teens, it was almost always teens, lost in a ravine on the other side of the island. It had rained heavily the day before, and with the tide high and the ponds and waterfalls full, the kids were soon stranded.

One teen had fallen and had nearly succumbed to his injuries before they could get him out and to the hospital. It was a harrowing flight back, in the twilight, knowing the boy hung by a thin strand of hope. He'd done these flights often but with trained men and women, not inexperienced youth with their entire life still ahead of them. They pronounced the young man dead upon arrival. Stopping to grab a bite to eat and some coffee, he went back out and picked up the last few not transported by the other helicopter and their rescuer.

It wasn't until after debriefing and taking care of his helicopter, had he allowed himself a moment to grieve the young life so senselessly lost. Chopper drove home, ready to crawl into his bed warmed by Felicity. Only when he came in, he saw she wasn't there. He was glad they had exchanged keys after the back door incident some weeks ago and had expected her car to be out front, but it wasn't. Maybe she just had someone drop her off straight from the flight to his house.

That twinge happened again, and he reached for his phone, but it was an ungodly hour to call her. She was likely exhausted like he was. He sent a text and told her he was back. That's when he noticed she hadn't read the last text. His gut churned with a warning.

Stand down, man. She's okay. You just talked to her last night, and if something had happened, you would have gotten a call. He'd made her change her next of kin to him. He prayed she did.

THE FOLLOWING DAY WHILE checking into her flight, the excitement was almost overwhelming, alleviating the fact that she had gotten little sleep. She kept reaching in her backpack to finger the envelope and to muse about the contents inside. It was so difficult to not open that folded paper. After touching it for the fiftieth time, she grabbed it and zipped the information inside the bag she placed on the cart and watched them take it over to the plane hold. That would keep her from opening it prematurely.

"Hey, Felicity? Doctor Torrez? The weather is still too close, so we won't take off for about twenty more minutes. I'm really sorry, especially since we couldn't get you out last night."

"That's okay. I'll just read and relax a little."

She grabbed the Cache Island News, and on the front page, she saw two pilots, and one was Darrell. She went on to read the story.

Search and rescue had located some reckless teens. One fatality. That's what her man was doing last night, and pride in who Darrell was, filled her with warmth. He never turned down a request for assistance if he had the means to help.

Someone touched her shoulder. "Ma'am?"

Felicity startled badly, her whole body shaking with the feeling of dread, even danger, but the man in front of her was anything but threatening. He wore neat, if worn, clothing and appeared clean, almost retiring. She should not hold it against the man that he had scared the crap out of her. She was too on edge. She wanted to get home to Darrell and attend to all the things they were working on.

She took a deep breath and let it out slowly. "Yes? Can I help you?" Her belly was still quivering. Calm down.

"Sorry to startle you, but I wonder if you could help me?"

"Oh, well, I don't know. I'm about to fly out." She scanned the room to see if anyone was in the little pre-boarding area. Nope. The desk was unmanned at the moment too. "What is it you need?"

"I had help to put my bag in the trunk, but I wonder if you could help me take it out. My back is still healing from an injury, so lifting and jerking aren't recommended. I looked around but couldn't find anyone to help."

"Yes, it takes a while to get back to normal. I'll be glad to help you." She put her backpack down under the seat and followed the man out.

AT SEVEN A.M., CHOPPER couldn't wait any longer. He had already gone to his place and found it empty. He grabbed his phone and called Felicity only to have it ring through to voice mail. He called the flight company.

"Inlet Air, this is Joe."

"Joe, Chopper here." His tone was all business.

"Hey man, how—"

"Joe, listen, I'm trying to find the Doc. Did you guys bring her back yesterday, or do you have any reservations for her today?"

"I don't think so, but let me check. No flights with her yesterday. Let me check today. Yes, she should be on this morning's first flight. Boarding in a few moments. I'll check the office over there to make sure she checked in. Hold on."

The two minutes he had to wait was almost more than Chopper could handle. He was mentally going through the preflight checklist to take off for the island himself. He was a man of action, and since he often was the transport, that had worked out well for his impatience. But not always. Like today. Waiting sucked.

He had just finalized the terms and put down the earnest money on that house across from Zed. Felicity had been as excited as he was to sign the paperwork to get things going. They were going over there with a contractor to agree on the few changes they needed before moving in. It was an unbelievable deal. Chopper and Felicity were pre-approved for well over the amount of the house, and the sale price was under appraisal by a goodly sum.

It was all working out for them, and he was going to propose before they took the co-ownership step. This weekend was going to be the time he gave her his ring. If he could get her to the altar before the house was theirs, that would be the best scenario. His gut clenched again.

"Chopper?" Joe's voice sounded more urgent now.

"Yeah?"

"She checked in but didn't board. Her bag was loaded, and they called her on the intercom, but she didn't answer. It's a little place, as you know. The only areas she could have been was in the parking lot or the bathroom, and both were checked before the plane took off. Maybe she got an emergency before she could leave?"

"Nah, she'd have told the counter agent and pulled her bag. I don't buy it. Will you check your cameras and call me if she shows back up?"

"You got it."

He called her phone again. No answer. He called the clinic, no Felicity and no emergencies that they were aware of. The next call was to Zed as he headed for his vehicle. Chopper was en route to his bird.

"Zayden Wellesley."

"Zed, thank fuck. We have a situation."

"I CALLED MY STATE TROOPER friend, and he said it's too early to file a missing person's report, but he did log it in that she was reported missing and that the family was beginning a search in earnest."

"Right," said River as he strode into Zed's house. Grabbing a cup of coffee, he looked at Chopper, who was pacing a hole in Zed's kitchen. "I'm ready to go wheels up and find Felicity. I brought my gear, and it will be much less hostile than Somalia or Paraguay. Piece of cake. We'll have your girl back in no time."

"Yeah, I know. My gut won't quit rioting until she's safe in my arms," said Chopper. "And I don't ever plan to let her go when I do."

Zed walked back into the room, followed by six trainers and six members of Zed's cold weather survival and extraction school. They were all highly trained special operatives, all intent on finding and extracting Felicity from whatever trouble she might be in.

"Alright, listen up. I got us two floatplanes for my group. River and I will fly over with you so we can strategize. We need to have a solid plan before we land so we don't lose time. Are we ready?"

Zed spoke to Brick, Johnny, and Cowboy, the only ones left from his original training team, giving them the low down on how things would go. Each made three teams of four. Ready to hit the ground once they get their orders from Zed, who was the command. River would run strategy since that was his forte, and it was both men's job to keep Chopper under control.

Once they were in the air, River started talking. "Okay, Zed, I think we move in the teams to cover the airport and surrounding area, the clinic, and the bed-and-breakfast she was in. They check in with you and follow the leads if they have any. Did we get any vehicles for transport?"

"I got us four, so that will give each team one," said Zed. "And don't worry about my guys. All we need to do is give them the game plan and turn them loose. They know this island pretty well and are all three the best."

River nodded. "Chopper. We are going to need you to help us with likely scenarios if we can't find her in these first three places."

Chopper's voice was rigid and stilted. "Roger that. The clinic is giving us her office to command from. She could be pregnant."

Zed unbuckled and moved up to one of the passenger seats next to his friend. "Man, listen to me. We will find her. No matter what, we will find her. And we won't stop until we do. You saved my life and my whole fucking family, so don't you think I'll do anything less for yours. Do you copy?"

"Copy that. Thanks, man, I know, it's just. Oh shit. I remember something. We need to know who Felicity's patients were on Wednesday. Older man. She said a neighbor to one of her patients, a retired Forest Service Ranger, had said that a man tried to kidnap a girl, late teens maybe, just recently. The Ranger told her it wasn't likely, but what if it did happen? What if they have a situation where he was foiled and tried again only was even bolder about it?"

"Could happen. I mean, if the would-be kidnapper was desperate or impatient, he might take that risk. And if he knew who she was and didn't know you two were together," Zed shrugged.

Chopper became animated. "And most wouldn't know about us because Doc doesn't live here, and she doesn't share about her personal life. She could be seen as an easy target. Living alone, about to leave, and no one would be the wiser for a few days. Monday. She had already turned in her bag to be loaded, and she had her pack. Damn."

River nodded. "We don't know that for sure, so don't put all your eggs in one basket, but it is a good lead and something we will absolutely check out."

Zed nodded his agreement. "I'll re-route the guys on Team One, Brick's team, to the clinic, and we will get that information from the staff and send them out with it. They can recon the area the attempted abduction was supposed to have happened earlier in the week. Team Two, Johnny's team, will check the airport and surrounding area. I still think that is a mandatory search area. Then Team Three, Cowboy's team, will hit the bed-and-breakfast she stays at."

River added. "We'll review the video footage and field reports. Talk to the girl's parents if we think it's a good idea."

"Landing in five," was all Chopper could say.

His woman was out there in the vast forest, alone. He was supposed to protect her. He scanned the area before landing. Doc knew her stuff, and it was the only thing that stopped him from roaring through the little village with a vengeance, breathing hellfire and brimstone destruction. Felicity wouldn't want that, but that was how he felt.

Once, while still in the service, Chopper saw a mother being dragged off from her little girl by some guerrillas. The men in his group saw red. They had just come off their last assignment and were to leave late that afternoon. He usually didn't mingle amongst the locals, and they kept a very low profile, but hell, not one of them could stomach this type of violence or walk away from it.

They had the little girl with the one team member who spoke the language. The other six of them headed into the ghetto after the screaming woman. Not one person attempted to help her, and that, alone, made Chopper determined to save her. They whispered a quick game plan, and everyone took their places, surrounding the kidnapper and the woman.

When they left to return the woman to her daughter, what was left of the man was unrecognizable, and he lay breathing but silent. Chopper's fury at the audacity of anyone touching his woman was the same as that feeling in a foreign country, times infinity. He could hardly contain it as he secured his helicopter and followed the others into the little building that housed the front desk.

Zed called for the vehicles, and River asking for Arne, the manager, as Chopper walked in. The counter clerk knew Chopper well and immediately apologized that she wasn't manning the desk when she disappeared.

"So you spoke to her?" asked Chopper asked hopefully.

"Yes, she was sitting right there." The clerk pointed to the only grouping of chairs in the little waiting area. She explained what she knew.

Chopper walked over there to see if he could find anything out of place. Anything that would lead him to Felicity, and then he saw it. Felicity shoved the little tan backpack she used as a purse far behind one seat against the wall.

It was nearly the color of the wall and small enough to be overlooked if one was just glancing over.

He leaned down and grabbed it. Just holding it in his hands cleared away the useless emotion tied to Doc's disappearance. Something had happened to her because she would not have left this behind. He channeled that inept emotion into sheer determination. Time to go get his girl.

"Found her pack," said Chopper, who walked to the counter and carefully began emptying every item from every pocket. Garbage and all. Nothing out of the ordinary. Not one thing he hadn't seen before, but the fact that her phone, wallet and tablet were still in there was enough to tell him she was somewhere she never expected to be and against her will.

"Nothing?" asked Zed as he came back inside with car keys.

"Nothing except that it is here at all. It has everything important in it. Where is that video?"

FELICITY HAD FOLLOWED the man and automatically watched his gait. It was awkward, so he likely did hurt his back. She didn't feel comfortable, but he said trunk, and she would be outside. They already knew she was flying out, so nothing would happen to her if she just helped him pull out the bag. As she waited for him to open the trunk, she realized that if he couldn't get it in or out of the trunk, how did he carry it to the car? He couldn't.

Searing pain shot through her head like a knife piercing her skull, and for a split second, she thought that was what had happened until she began to feel her entire head vibrate. Her mind was scrambling to grasp what was happening, and then everything went dark. Had she passed out? No, she was still thinking.

Lying still so she could settle her body's reaction and hopefully avoid unconsciousness or shock, Felicity forced herself to slow her breathing and calm her erratic thoughts. Now, what is my plan to get out of this situation? Where was a Special Ops team strategist when you needed him, she thought as the wave of nausea overtook her.

She was in the trunk of that car, and her head pounded, her stomach roiled. She was still in danger of passing out. Think about what it would take for someone to know someone took her against her will. Chopper would have expected her last night, so even if he just went home and fell asleep, he would have noticed her gone by at least this morning. Good. That would mean when the plane landed, and she wasn't on it, and then he couldn't get hold of her, he would come guns blazing because that's how that man was with her these days.

Everything with Chopper was more intense, and his ability to read situations was just as good as anyone on Zed's training team or River Bennett's expertise. Better because he loved her. And she might be carrying his child. Remembering that possibility sobered her thinking and solidified her goals. Time to figure this out. She'd have to hide or at least stay alive until Chopper found her. There were no other choices, so she waited for her opportunity.

Felicity realized she had lost consciousness, but she instinctively knew they had been driving for a long time. This was an expansive island, littered with little pockets of people who lived all over. You would never know they were there unless you stumbled on them or knew about them. There were four villages of under a thousand people, and then there was everyone else. Getting help would be difficult if she didn't know the area they were in.

She'd just have to rely on her training to keep her alive and Chopper and the guys' training to find her. She had no doubt he had a group helping him because that was what their little community was all about, teamwork and support. She hoped it was enough.

Chapter 12

Zed gave the orders to the teams, but it was apparent to the little group that the overall leadership had changed hands since finding Felicity's pack. Chopper was in the zone, and he was thinking fast. It's precisely where he should be to make this rescue work.

"I don't care what you think. I know for an absolute fact that there is a security camera running at all times in this place. I was told it was regulations by your boss himself."

The office manager was suddenly awfully skittish. "Chopper," said River, "I remember you saying something to me about that friend you have in the FAA, that pilot who took an office job to monitor little airfields. Who was that?"

Catching River's intent, Chopper replied. "Right, I forgot about old Iron Fist. Did I ever tell you he broke a table in the mess hall when he found out they ran out of steak? The man had balls."

Chopper could hear and feel the employee beside him vibrate. "Now, that is not necessary. I'll call the owner again."

"Don't bother," said Zed as he crossed the room. "I just spoke to him, and he said he'd be here in ten minutes." Zed turned to Arne. "Evidently, you haven't spoken to him today."

"What? But I have." The now sweating man looked at the clerk. "Linda, you heard me on the phone."

"I did, but I don't know who you were talking to." Chopper's opinion of the clerk rose as she refused to put herself in the middle of something she could likely feel was going explode any second.

Arne went back into the offices. Chopper didn't have time for him. Let his boss deal with the fool, but why was he lying to them? They sat down for a moment before a door in the back shut. Chopper jumped over the counter and ran full hilt to where the office manager had left. Joe, the site owner/operator, pulled into the parking lot as Arne was peeling out.

Zed grabbed his arm. "The clerk said the camera is still working, so nothing for him to hide. River is already working on getting the footage we need cued up." Zed got an update from his teams and followed Chopper in the office that seemed smaller with four men in it, three of which were much larger than average.

"Okay, I have this set up and ready to go from six a.m. to whenever."

Chopper shook the owner's hand. "Thanks, Joe. I really appreciated this."

"Hell, if it were my wife or daughter, I'd be burning down the town looking for them."

"I'm exercising restraint. Zed here says what we do has to be legal." A ghost of a smile crossed Joe's lips before it disappeared. The video began, and they set it for 2x speed and watched intently. They saw a man arrive, and Arne went out to speak to him. Then the manager went inside, and the man drove away.

"Hey, I think I know that man. Let me think a minute, and I'll remember."

The video continued. Felicity arrived, and Chopper's knees almost gave out. They watched the whole thing and saw the same man again, this time coming inside then going up to Felicity to speak with her. Doc looked around and then nodded, placing her bag under the seat and left the building.

"Do you have footage of the parking lot?"

"Yes. Hold on. Linda, come and look at this man. See if you recognize him," asked Joe.

Linda came in, and River backed it up to show the stranger. "Sure, that's Arne's uncle. You know, the man who lost his wife about six months ago?"

Chopper shot out the question harshly. "Where does he live?"

"He's a nice guy, just lonely. Oh, you don't think...?"

"Where does he live?" demanded Chopper.

"No idea. Not in town."

"Got the feed set up," said River. And they watched the whole kidnapping. Mud obliterated the tags on the car.

Zed spoke at the end of the video. "I just put in a call to my trooper friend and filled him in. He's going to call over and get Arne picked up. In the meantime, we need to regroup. I'm pulling the guys in. As soon as we know where the man lives, we will go there. Until then, we figure out what we do once we are there. This is how I see it."

THE CAR WAS FINALLY slowing down, and it looked to be turning off the road they had been on. That meant further from the primary access road and harder to find. They stopped, and she heard a door open but not close. The man who had tricked her into the car was speaking to someone. There were two?

"They can't have her back, Arne. I told you I needed a woman. I can't function with Rita gone."

"It doesn't matter, and I don't care if she has a hotshot military boyfriend. And I don't care that they have brought a small army of guys with them. They won't find me, and I need her more than he does. She's a doctor, too. Isn't that great luck?"

The talking seemed to get further and further away until she thought her opportunity wouldn't be any better to get away. Chopper and company were in town, and evidently, someone knew both sides of this story. An accomplice. She reached for the lever in the back of the trunk and thanked God the man bought American this century cars.

Ever so slowly, she pulled the lever, and the back popped open. She opened it enough to look out, and as she scanned the area, she saw the back of her kidnapper, peeing on a tree and still talking on the phone. She ignored her head and nausea, and as much as she could, the dizziness as she quickly but as quietly as possible, got out of the trunk.

As gently as she could, she closed the back, so it just clicked closed. It sounded as loud as anything she had ever known. She looked back to check the man, and he was zipping his trousers and still talking. No time to waste. Felicity sprinted to the surrounding woods and tried to ignore her head pounding. She didn't wait to see if he realized she had slipped away from him. She just kept going.

Soon she heard the car start up, and it sounded like it was driving away. Good. He didn't know she was no longer in the trunk. She looked for a hiding spot so she could recuperate and think of what to do next. When her kidnapper was long gone, she went back the other way, listening hard as she went. It wouldn't do for her to escape, only to be recaptured.

After walking for a short while, she had to sit again, going less and less distance between the need for a break. Felicity was sick and exhausted because of her concussion, and it was getting harder and harder to continue. She was glad for her jacket with its detachable hood that she could use for a modified pillow and lay on a pile of leaves and pine needles with more of the same covering her as a kind of camouflage. Then she closed her eyes.

ZED SAID. "THEY HAVE Charles Lockland in custody, but when they opened the trunk where Felicity was supposed to be, it was empty. The man doesn't know where she is. He didn't believe the troopers until he looked himself, that she was even gone. He lost it, and they had to restrain him. The troopers believe he really doesn't know where she is. In his efforts to figure out where she was, thinking he still had a chance to keep her, he began rambling about stopping someplace, but it's just a guess."

"Fucker," said Chopper under his breath as he grabbed his gear. "Okay, we know the road he left on by the video and can put in the coordinates to Lockland's house. A little calculation gives us a general area she is likely to be in. It's still an expanse. Two teams start that end. The remaining team with us."

River continued. "We go a klick before where the last place his phone pinged, praying that's where she got out. We work toward the first two teams and meet in the middle. Remember, she may be a doctor, but she was an Army doctor, so that means she has skills."

"Thank God for that," said River.

Zed "Yes, but it will be harder to find her because she's hurt. She likely took cover. To what extent, we can't be sure, but I think we can assume she has one helluva headache and equally likely a concussion."

"That would slow her down. I'm worried that with a hit on the head like we witnessed in the parking lot, she might be passed out somewhere." Chopper felt his inner cramp at the thought, but it stoked his momentum even more.

They all disbursed to their locations and began the search. It was a slow, tedious process to call for Felicity, stop, listen for any response or rustle of vegetation, walk a little further and repeat the same routine. After working a while, Teams One and Two were taking a brief break.

"We need to take a break as well, Chopper. We can't afford to miss her, so we have to give them a few moments to regroup. I want to look at the way we're doing things. The sun is almost gone, and the clouds are blocking the full moon, which is close but muted because of the drizzle. That is going to make it more likely to miss her if we aren't taking breaks to refresh and regroup." Zed was not relenting on this point.

Chopper turned and yelled back. "I'm not stopping. I didn't think you would either; not so soon." The hard resentment was loud in his words and tone.

"Hell, no, we aren't quitting. No man left behind, remember? She is out here and one of ours, so we are absolutely going to find her, but we're going to have a harder time of it now," reasoned River. "Here is my thinking. You fire up the helicopter, and I'll go up with you. Zed, you stick with your teams. Give them a dinner break until we get back. I'm glad we had the forethought to keep the vehicles with us as we searched. Have your guys head back here. And wait for us." He turned to Chopper. "I know you have a searchlight on your bird."

"Hot damn. Yes. We'll head back, and I'll get us airborne. We'll search from the sky."

FELICITY OPENED HER eyes and tried to stifle her cry of pain without much success. Her head pounded, and without pain relievers and fluids, she wasn't going to find any relief soon. She laid still and tried to bring her brain back online. Her thoughts sought and found the events that got her under these leaves in this ravine. And it was dark. Given the time of year and the level of darkness, it had to be really late. No wonder she felt a faint gnawing in her belly not associated with the crack on her head.

She tried to move, and her nausea returned full force. *She'd hoped that Chopper would have found her by now, but she imagined she was hidden pretty well. Remember your training, and don't give in to fear. At least if Chopper hasn't found you,* "Mr. help me with my bag," *won't either.*

She looked around very carefully, but before she could attempt to pull herself upright gingerly, she heard a rustle of leaves and the shuffle of the loose vegetation on the forest floor. It was slight, but she heard it, telling her it was an animal of some kind. Whether two-legged or four, she wasn't sure yet. The moon's light was diminished by the cloud cover. Any assistance the night sky might have given in seeing the landscape and animals around her was gone. She listened longer.

Male voices. A streak of fear vibrated through Felicity's entire body. She shivered and nearly gagged, forcing herself to take slow deep breaths to get things to stop moving. She held position and waited.

"Felicity? We're here to take you home," the voice said.

But she didn't recognize that voice. It could be the kidnapper. She stayed silent and as still as she could. She needed to go pee, but that would have to wait.

"Felicity, can you hear me, darlin'?"

Had she heard that twangy voice before? Something in the back of her mind told her she might recognize that voice. They walked off in another direction. Unable to hold the contents of her bladder any longer, Felicity shuffled ever so carefully to the part of the ravine with more exposed dirt and dropped her pants. The relief helped her aching belly but not entirely. She knew only too well that she might have a head bleed. She needed a hospital.

Was that someone else coming close? Was that an animal? She leaned forward slightly to hear better, and a flash of stadium-grade light covered the ground she was sitting on. Another rustle, and she couldn't move fast enough to get out of the way before she was touched on the shoulder.

Forgetting her head was a fishbowl full of fire, she turned and rolled out of the way. The edges of her sight were darkening. Her peripheral vision was reducing fast. She vomited the remaining acid in her stomach.

"Felicity, it's Zed. Alli's husband." To his credit, he didn't touch her right away. "Come on, honey, you're in a bad way."

She processed a few seconds longer than one would expect before she released a sob. "Zed, thank God." She promptly dry heaved. "Zed here. I've got her, Chopper. Repeat. The target has been located and recovered."

He spoke to someone else, and then she found herself lifted up out of the landmine of bodily fluids and without so much as a word, he carried her to a road where she was laid very gently on the back seat of a vehicle. She could hear Zed talking to Cowboy. The twang. She should have realized it wasn't her kidnapper because he didn't have much of an accent at all. Almost flat. Depressed. Why hadn't she realized that before?

Zed was speaking again. "You're coming with me. I need you to ride back with River and Chopper to monitor our girl here. I'll drop you off and come back for a few of the guys. We're a vehicle short to return."

"Sir," said Johnny as he closed the distance between himself and the two men with Felicity. "We have two SUVs, and the men are willing to use the back of the vehicle to ride to the plane dock."

"Right. Well, tell you what, the teams are yours and Brick's. If you can get them home and settled for the night, there is a three-day weekend in it for you all. Do call me if you have any trouble. You good with that?"

"Aye, sir."

Zed nodded to Johnny, turned away, and jumped behind the wheel. "We good, Cowboy?"

"All good, sir. Felicity is passed out again, but that's preferable to being awake and feeling every bump in the road. I gave her a little pain reliever, but with not knowing the extent of her injuries, I'm limited on what I can offer."

"Just keep her as stable as you can. I'll get us to Chopper."

"Did you hear what I said to Johnny back there?"

"Some of it."

"Same goes for you. Just help me keep the peace with her man, and get Felicity to the hospital, then you're released until Monday."

"Do we have time to do that, Zed?"

"Yep, we do. That end of training mission we were going to do in about ten days? We just did it. We'll spend Monday debriefing and talking out the good, the bad, and the ugly. Then we'll write it up and file it away."

"Sounds good."

They had gone a fair distance, so it took some time to arrive back at the little village and the Isle Air loading dock. Chopper was pacing the parking lot and nearly jumped them before the car stopped moving.

Chopper hadn't been in the air for long before his spotlight seemed to hit something shiny. Zed had stepped into the light and walked in its path, going forward. Then he jumped ahead, and the next man who stepped in his light looked like Brick, who gave Chopper the mission accomplished sign, and as he backed off, a message was relayed to Chopper and River from the floatplane company. Good to go. They found Felicity and were bringing her in. Darrell thought he could finally breathe.

Jerking open the door, Chopper dropped to his knees, reaching where her head was on the seat and gently cradled it. "Oh, baby. I'm so sorry I left you. I hate you had this happen to you. I'm so damn sorry. You aren't going anywhere alone for a very long time." He looked up at Cowboy. "Is she passed out or sleeping hard?"

"A little of both, actually. I worry about her head. We need a CT scan AS-AP."

Zed tapped Chopper on the shoulder. "Help me get her in the terminal. We need to assess her again in the light and then get her to the hospital in Point Refuge. We can explain everything on the way."

Chopper jumped up and pushed his devastation to the back of his brain. He was no longer the man who was heartbroken over his girlfriend's traumatic injury and the recent horrors. He was the extraction team and the protector of his woman. He had her in his arms, but until he had her cleared by medical personnel, she was still in danger. That was unacceptable.

Chopper took a second to think of how she would have teased him for thinking she needed a protector before this incident, but if she were to stay conscious long enough, he would tell her to relax; he knew how this went. He could handle this role. It was who he wanted to be forever, her shield against the evil of the world.

When they strode into the flight building, a doctor and nurse had just landed back in town after their wedding and short honeymoon. They met the group with Felicity, and there were some supplies he had told them to have on hand. His office supplied them, and they were there at the ready.

"She seems exhausted, and I would imagine a little dehydrated. I'd get a CT of her head. I'm not sure how much damage there was, but she definitely has a concussion. Her eyes are reactive, so that's good. Do I need to go over with you?" The man seemed reluctant, and Chopper understood.

"No, we have our field Medic here, and he's going back anyway, so no need to take you away from your bride."

Chopper turned to scoop the love of his life in his arms and started for the helicopter. Felicity stirred, and Darrell's voice, low and rich like aged scotch, spoke to her. "I love you, Felicity. I've got you, honey. You're safe now, so just relax, okay?"

"Darrell? I love you. I don't feel well."

"I know, honey, but we are getting you fixed up in no time. Okay?"

"Okay." She closed her eyes again.

Zed and Cowboy jumped inside ahead of them so they could take her from Chopper's arms and settle her. Chopper had gotten out all his blankets, a pillow, and a sleeping bag from his Go-Bag behind the seats. They were all ready to go inside of five minutes as Chopper had his preflight checks done. He did his last re-checks while his friends took care of Felicity.

River stayed behind to get his law firm involved. He had chartered one large floatplane back home as it was after the last flight of the evening, and there were no hotels to house the group. The plane was ready to go when they were; River made sure of it. The rescue group left the cars at the Inlet Air parking lot for pick up the next morning, and the loose ends were all tied up for now.

Once in the air, Zed explained how they found Felicity. "She taught us a valuable lesson. Several, actually. She heard Cowboy calling her name, and she didn't know his voice, so she feared she had been found by the wrong people. When she heard my voice, it was okay."

Cowboy looked up from checking on Felicity. "She's coming around again. You need to talk, Chopper, so she doesn't panic. I placed her so she can see you without much movement."

"Here, this is her headset." He reached his arm behind him, and Zed grabbed the device.

"I don't know how well she'll tolerate it but just long enough to know you are near."

Zed placed the headset so one speaker was against her ear and positioned the mic near her mouth. "Talk to her."

"Felicity, hi sweetheart. You're safe now. We're in the helicopter, and we'll be at the hospital in a few minutes."

"Chopper?" came her sweet voice, quiet and wistful. "Is it really you?" her voice was thick, and she had trouble speaking. "I don't feel well. I should go to the hospital."

"You are going. We'll be landing in about ten more minutes. I called them, and the helipad is free for now. I love you."

Her dry lips were still covered with a film of dirt, as was most of her, but Darrell Frazier still thought she was the most beautiful woman in the world.

"I love you, too." She closed her eyes again.

Epilogue

Felicity looked over at Darrell now and smiled. For the first time, she had not felt so tired and could stay awake for longer than a few minutes. The sun was up, and she looked at the board. It was the next morning after she had been kidnapped. The mere memory made her tremble, but looking down at Darrell, who was sitting in a chair next to her bed, she felt so very blessed. She was well medicated, rehydrated, and rested enough. He had one hand holding hers and the other laying protectively over her belly. His head was on the bed as he napped. She moved a smidgen, and he jumped.

"Baby? Are you okay? Do you need anything? Anything hurt? I'll call the nurse."

"I'm good, Darrell, I'm good. I'm not perfect yet, but I'm good."

"There, you're wrong because you are perfect. My perfect lady. Can you tell me what happened?"

A voice behind them, kind but authoritative, said, "I'd rather she tell me, and you listen if you don't mind." The Alaska State Trooper put out his hand to Felicity. "I'm Trooper Tristan Hart, Doctor Torrez. Do you feel up to answering a few questions about yesterday?"

"Sure, and call me Felicity."

Trooper Hart shook hands with Felicity and then turned to shake Chopper's hand. "And you are Darrell Frazier, the pilot, also known as Chopper."

"That's me. You're Zayden's trooper friend. Good to meet you."

"Likewise. Now, Felicity, tell me what you remember." After fifteen minutes, Tristan was leaving, promising to keep in touch. "And don't worry about Charles Lockland or his nephew Arne. They are safely behind bars."

"Thank you."

As they sat there for a few moments, quietly talking, Felicity's face became animated. "Oh, the results are in my bag."

"What results? Oh, right. What were they?"

"I don't know. I put them in the bag so that I wouldn't be tempted to open the envelope without you."

"Honey, I'm sorry, but they must be lost because it wasn't in your backpack."

She smiled. "Nope, they are in the bag I had put in the hold."

"Ah, well, you're in luck. They delivered that here this morning." He stood to get the bag in the corner and opened it to pull out a white envelope.

"They did? Why?"

"Joe's pretty worried you will sue. It was his manager over there that helped make your abduction possible."

"I just can't get my head around it." They were silent for a few seconds. "But we can finally see the results."

"Wait. Before we know if you are pregnant or not, I want you to hear me out. Felicity, I have loved you since the moment you made me laugh on the helicopter ride over to save lives. I was impressed with your candor, your professionalism, and expertise. I was especially impressed with your skills in putting mouthing men in their place. And in the mess tent, you showed you could be submissive but still hold your head up and demand respect, and that is a fucking turn-on. You had me hooked."

"I was enthralled with you and still am."

"Felicity Torrez, you are perfect for me. You are intelligent and strong-willed but have so much compassion that I sometimes worry that it will get you into trouble. And it has, making me crazy, but I know if you weren't, I wouldn't be as attracted to you. I love you, sweetheart, with all that I am. Will you marry me, and if we aren't pregnant, have my children, share my life and allow me to share yours?"

Tears were rolling down Felicity's face, and she had a look of pure adoration that he would never forget. "Yes, I'll marry you."

"No more fears of messing things up?"

She smiled again. "Oh, I still worry about that, but you have shown me that you won't let anything get between us. Not kidnappers, not self-sabotage. How could I not be in love with a man who likes control a little too much but easily gives it to me if I ask for it? One who comes to my rescue without being asked and who treats me as though I am special in so many little ways. Yes, you're bossy, but I think I can handle that because you're also possessive, protective, and giving to me, to the community, your friends, to everyone."

"Not those assholes who set you up and took you."

"No, but that's because you have morals, scruples, that they don't have. And thank you for not killing anyone. I know you could have easily."

Chopper grunted. "It was hard."

She put her hand on his. "I know. Now can we open the envelope?"

"Hell, yes."

She opened it excitedly but with careful fingers. "Guess the equipment works. You're going to be a father." She grinned widely as Darrell squeezed her tight and just as quickly let her go when she made a noise of discomfort.

"A father. That's incredible."

The attending physician walked in. "Hello, you two. I have what I hope is great news. You're pregnant."

Felicity laughed. "Yes, we know."

IT HAD BEEN TWO WEEKS since Felicity was kidnapped and ten days since she had come home from the hospital. Her concussion had been a grade 3 with a bleed that was manageable but worrisome. After four days, they had released her because she was a doctor and knew the signs of trouble.

During the whole hospital stay, Darrell had stuck with her like flypaper and nothing, and no one was going to move him until she was released. That made Felicity all warm and fuzzy inside, and as she got better, all hot and bothered as well.

In that short span of time, she had put in her notice for her cottage, changed her job in that she only stayed on Cache Island. Jans and Janis had grown close with the newlyweds on the other island and had agreed to finish their contract, another two years, doing the island work exclusively, and she would not go again. They would give her support as needed until a male nurse practitioner could be found and was relocated to Cache Island. That went amazingly far in Chopper relaxing his push for her to find another way to practice her medicine, and she was able to let much of the worry go as well.

The arrangement had been blessedly easy, and Darrell made changes at his work as well. His boss would retire from operating the business and gave that part over to Chopper. If he decided he liked that position, after two years, he could buy the company. Her man was over the moon with that kind of opportunity. He immediately hired a pilot he'd known in the military that was getting out in a matter of weeks. He was single and like Chopper not long ago, looking for a change he could settle into.

Because Chopper wasn't single anymore. He and Felicity had gotten married in front of Jenn, Kayla, River, Alli, and Zed as their witnesses. They were going to have a small get-together in their honor, now that she hadn't had a headache for four days. Felicity felt well enough that next week she would go back to half days at work. Her dizziness was resolved, and that should have stopped her nausea, but she still had some, although this nausea didn't worry her. She took ginger and saltine crackers everywhere.

Sitting in chairs at Zed and Alli's place, they gazed over at the new house Felicity and Chopper had signed for and were waiting on the upgrades to happen before moving in.

"I can't believe you have done all of this in such a short time. Zed is always complaining that I leap into things too quickly. I mean, not one thing isn't changing in your world," said Alli.

"I know. It can be scary at times, but Darrell says we are forging a new land."

"Honey, you are pioneering a new country. I can't imagine what Zed said to Chopper when he found out about all this upheaval."

Zed leaned in from behind Alli and kissed the top of her head. "I told him it was too much too soon. Then I said he was one lucky son of a bitch. And it was about damn time he got with the program."

The women laughed.

"And I agreed," said Chopper as he leaned down to drop a kiss on Felicity's lips. "Who would have ever guessed that the best tactical decision of my life was to take a female Army Doc to help do triage in the field on her last day in country."

Felicity smiled. "Mmm, who would have guessed, indeed."

The End

About the Author
Alyssa Bailey

USA Today and #1 Bestselling Author of Diverse Romance that is realistic and sensual with a touch of suspense. A dyed in the wool Texan living in Alaska for half her life, Alyssa now divides her time between the beauty of Southeast Alaska and the piney woods of East Texas. She enjoys taking from her own experiences to create series in fictitious worlds that are sure to tease the reader's palate and invite them to sink into exciting adventures.

Alyssa enjoys writing consensual power exchanges between intelligent, sassy women who are not afraid to make a stand and loving men confident enough to give his woman space but masterful enough to keep her safe despite her choices. There is *always* a happily ever after.

Visit me online and sign up for my Newsletter:
http://alyssabailey.com[1]
Join my Facebook Group for fun and prizes:
https://www.facebook.com/alyssabailey.romance

---

1. http://alyssabailey.com/

Other Romance Books by Alyssa Bailey

Lords and Little Ladies: Georgian Historical, spicy

Lord Thayer's Choice

Lord Ashton's Decision

The Black Laird Requires

Lord Kendrick's Obligation

Darling Duchesses: Regency, Daddy Dom, Spicy

The Devil Duke's Little Distraction (May 2021)

Chase Abbey Series: Regency, Spicy, Suspense

Lord Barrington's Minx

Becoming Lady Barrington

Lady Caroline's Defiance

His Improper Lady

Safe and Secure Series: Contemporary, suspense, spicy

Saving Sharlee

Saving Jessie

Safe and Secure II: Contemporary, Suspense, Spicy

Saving Ivy

Securing Mallory (2021)

Securing Becky (2021)

Securing Finley (TBD)

Securing Callie (TBD)

The O'Connor Series: Contemporary, Rancher, Saga, Spicy

Liam & Jocelyn's Story-

Her Sweet Complication

Liam's Lessons

Loving Liam

Ciarán and Katherine's Story

His Gentle Persuasion

Rancher's Creed

Katie Consents

Quinlan and Cheyenne's Story

Quinlan's Quest

Accepting His Way

Her Balancing Act
Kelli and Parker's Story
Meeting Her Needs
Kissing Kelli
Keeping Kelli
Cián and Molly's Story
In Pursuit of Molly
Freeing Molly
Forever Molly
Clearwater Ranch Trilogy -Contemporary, Spicy
Piper's Plan
Camille's Second Chance
Josie's Refuge
Lone Wind Series: Contemporary, spicy Native American
Reclaiming Clover
Taming Texanna -American Historical, Native American, Spicy
Cowboy Welcome- Contemporary, Spicy
In the Spirit of Christmas -Contemporary, Sweet
Guardians of Refuge (Contemporary, Military, Spicy)
SEAL of Refuge
The Strategy of Love
The Tactics of Love

ANTHOLOGIES (HEAT VARIES)

Sweet Town Love
Historical Heroes
Hero to Obey (limited time)
Cowboy for a Cause (limited time)

MULTI-AUTHOR BOX SETS (Heat Level Various)

Love, Christmas 2 Movies You Love
Love, Christmas 2 Recipes

FREE Book Bites 11
Christmas Shorts
Irresistible Heroes
Tempting Protectors
Sexy and Seductive
Sweet and Sassy Summertime Vol. 2
Dear Santa: A Christmas Wish
Sweet and Sassy New Beginnings

Don't miss out!

Visit the website below and you can sign up to receive emails whenever Alyssa Bailey publishes a new book. There's no charge and no obligation.

https://books2read.com/r/B-A-MXIL-VERPB

BOOKS 2 READ

Connecting independent readers to independent writers.

Did you love *The Tactics of Love*? Then you should read *SEAL of Refuge* by Alyssa Bailey!

Too Good To Be True

Alesha Campbell loves her Alaskan island home but two years after a painful break up, she fears she might be terminally single. Then she meets the new guy in town. The widowed Naval officer extricates her from a sticky situation and stole her heart, but he seems too good to be true. That's because he is.

When the Navy offers SEAL Commander Zayden Wellesley the career opportunity of a lifetime, he accepts. On a recon trip to his new station, he meets the woman he never knew he needed and sets about wooing her. Things are going well over the short trip except for one little snag: He neglected to inform her he had roommates.

Zed did plan to tell Alli before she found out on her own, however, his roommates took matters into their own hands before he could talk to her. Can Zayden save his career and his budding relationship without upsetting the delicate balance he was already maintaining?

Read more at alyssabailey.com.

Also by Alyssa Bailey

Guardians of Refuge
The Tactics of Love

Red Eagle Ranch
Stryker's Girl

Watch for more at alyssabailey.com.